30 JAN 2020

SH

Richmond upon Thames Libraries

Renew online at www.richmond.gov.uk/libraries

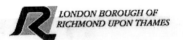

LONDON BOROUGH OF
RICHMOND UPON THAMES

Praise for *The International Yeti Collective*:

"[...] an absolute delight! Warm and wise and wonderfully whiffy (exactly how I imagine a yeti-hug)."
– Sophie Anderson, author of *The House With Chicken Legs*

"As a biologist, I can neither confirm nor deny the existence of yeti. To do so would endanger them the world over. This book taps into the secret lives of our mythical and very hairy cousins and takes us on an adventure like no other. Tick and his hairy friends show us what it means to work together and why we need to save the world."
– Professor Ben Garrod, author of *The Chimpanzee and Me*

"By turns funny, moving, and action-packed, *The International Yeti Collective* is a fast-moving adventure with a meditative, philosophical heart. Perfect for fans of H.S. Norup's *The Missing Barbegazi*."
– Sinéad O'Hart, author of *The Eye of the North*

"The kind of book you wish your parents had read to you as a child. An emotionally intelligent, absorbing adventure that carries at its heart the most wonderful message of being at one with nature. Y5/6 will adore it. Are you YETI for this?"
– Scott Evans, @MrEPrimary

"[...] an excellent story, mixing cryptozoology and conservation themes with some lovely characters and its own fantastic mythology."
– Liam James, @notsotweets

"A delightful tale of yeti, bravery and protecting nature. This is a fast-paced, heart-warming adventure."
– Erin Hamilton, @erinlynhamilton

PAUL MASON

KATY RIDDELL

THE
INTERNATIONAL
YETI
COLLECTIVE

Stripes

STRIPES PUBLISHING LIMITED
An imprint of the Little Tiger Group
1 Coda Studios, 189 Munster Road,
London SW6 6AW

www.littletiger.co.uk

First published in Great Britain by Stripes Publishing Limited in 2019
Text copyright © Paul Mason, 2019
Illustrations copyright © Katy Riddell, 2019

Quote from Gerald Durrell produced with permission of Curtis Brown Group Ltd,
London on behalf of The Beneficiaries of the Estate of Gerald Durrell.
Copyright © Gerald Durrell

ISBN: 978-1-78895-084-8

A CIP catalogue record for this book is available from the British Library.

Printed and bound in the UK.

The Forest Stewardship Council® (FSC®) is a global, not-for-profit organization
dedicated to the promotion of responsible forest management worldwide. FSC defines
standards based on agreed principles for responsible forest stewardship that are supported
by environmental, social, and economic stakeholders. To learn more, visit www.fsc.org

2 4 6 8 10 9 7 5 3 1

For Jenny
– PM

For William and Jack
– KR

I've spent a great deal of my life searching deep into the wilderness and, in the end, I am no closer to finding yeti than when I began. But perhaps that's just as well. What if I had discovered yeti? What then?

Ray Stevens, 1971

Ella Stern stopped and peered into the rolling mist. She was sure she'd heard a crackle in the forest, a snapping of twigs. She held her breath and for a moment all was silent and still on the mountainside, then once again she heard the rip and crunch of leaves. There was a dark shape hiding in the trees ahead. She tried to call Uncle Jack but nothing came out.

A gentle breath of wind wafted over the mountains and a gap cleared in the mist, revealing a small dark face peering from a low branch, and a long tail dangling below. Ella laughed. It was a monkey – a langur. For a moment, she had actually thought she'd encountered a yeti. She'd already written the headline: Twelve-Year-Old Girl Discovers Existence of Mythical Creature – Worldwide Sensation!

Ella raised her camera and rattled off a couple of quick

shots as the monkey stuffed handfuls of leaves into its mouth, managing to capture the moment before it sprang off further into the forest. She couldn't wait to share all the photos with April and her other friends when she got back home to New Zealand.

Once she was sure the monkey had gone, she turned away, following the river back to camp. She passed the dense rhododendron trees, their flowers a blaze of colour even in the fading afternoon light, and then she was close enough to hear the crackle of the campfire and see its glow flickering over the tents. Uncle Jack sat on a log, holding his hands to the flames, chatting to Ana the director about tomorrow's film shoot. Walker fiddled with one of his video cameras and listened.

Near the tents the yak grazed – curved horns lowered, tails swishing. Ella brought her camera to her eye again – she wanted to hold this moment and keep it forever. Here she was, up in the Himalayas, about as far away from home as it was possible to get.

When her parents had first suggested she spend the holidays on location with her TV-star uncle, Ella had actually been a little unsure. She rarely saw Uncle Jack – he was always off in the wilderness, filming something or other. Ella loved his shows. There was *Stern Stuff*, where Uncle Jack survived the plains of Africa, living with a group of cheetahs. Then came the carnivorous plants series in the Amazon, *From Stem to Stern*, and her favourite: *Stern Times*, the polar adventure where he marched with the penguins. Uncle Jack cared about wildlife, and Ella knew if she came on this trip, it would be a great chance to get close to the animals herself. Not to mention this was the first time Jack had ever tried to film something as legendary as a yeti. Besides, she'd finally got the digital camera she'd been saving and saving for. What better place to use it?

In the end, Ella had a choice – a summer stuck at home with sitters, while her parents made one business trip after another, or an expedition deep into the Himalayas on *Jack Stern: Yeti Quest*. No contest. And what if Uncle Jack actually found a yeti? Now that would be incredible.

On the trek to their campsite, Uncle Jack had told her all about his passion for yeti. Before the trip, Ella hadn't been at all convinced they were real, but, after listening to her uncle, she was beginning to change her mind. Uncle Jack told her how the people in the mountains knew yeti as 'wild men'; that some thought yeti could be a species of giant ape, long believed extinct; how an expedition paid for by a famous newspaper discovered a footprint in the mud the length of a pickaxe; that it was rumoured yeti liked to sneak into mountain villages at night to steal cattle if they could.

Jack also told her the story of a famous yeti sighting

by an explorer called Ray Stevens. Stevens had taken the first-ever photo of the mythical beast, but later it was pronounced a fake. According to Jack, Ray Stevens spent the rest of his life in disgrace.

"But that's not going to happen to me!"

As they had trekked, Uncle Jack constantly consulted a little black journal, checking his notes and looking at the map, then finally announcing they were getting closer to yeti habitat.

Ella turned her gaze from the campsite and looked around the mountains. What if Uncle Jack was right and they *were* close to yeti land? What would it even look like? Were there yeti right here, hiding in the forest? Could they be up higher, where the mountains looked like crumpled paper bags? Or further away still, where the highest peaks gleamed, bright with snow?

A shout broke into her thoughts. "Hey, Ella, how's that firewood coming? We're almost out."

Firewood. Ella looked down at her empty hands.

"Just a sec, Uncle Jack!" she called back. Ella fixed the lens cap back on to her camera and started gathering twigs. By the time she reached the others, she had an armload, which she dumped by the fire.

"Guess what? I spotted a langur!" said Ella. She showed them the display on her camera.

"You're getting good at those wildlife shots," said

Uncle Jack with a smile.

"Nice," said Ana.

"So, to wrap things up," Jack continued, feeding some wood into the fire, "we'll start with the establishing shots in the morning – I want you to really set the scene, Walker. Remote base camp in the Himalayas … Jack Stern, hot on the heels of the yeti … risking life and limb, et cetera."

"I could get some long-range shots from downriver, with the mountain backdrop," suggested Walker, rubbing his beard.

"Perfect," said Jack. He switched on his torch and opened his little black journal, tracing a line on a hand-drawn diagram with his finger, then comparing it to his map. "And then, if there's still time on the first day, I reckon we leave the yak behind and explore the forest south of here on foot, trekking down towards the valley."

"That could work," said Ana, studying the map.

"Then we head off from camp on day treks, a different route each time. If any particular location looks promising, we can shift base."

"Sounds like a plan, Jack," agreed Walker.

"Can I help?" asked Ella.

Ana got to her feet. "Sure, you can start by giving me a hand setting up the night-vision cameras. I'd like to get them in place before we lose any more daylight. See if we can capture any nocturnal activity."

"Great," said Ella.

While Walker checked that the little black boxes were charged, Ana pointed at the trees above their camp. "Walker, you set up a couple in the woods just above us while Ella and I go across the river. I like the look of the area near that rocky ledge."

Ella and Ana crossed the river at its shallowest point, stepping from stone to stone, and then climbed the riverbank. Ana chose a nearby tree and showed Ella how to fasten a band round the trunk, clip on the camera box and switch it on.

"Now tie one of those cloth markers to a branch so we can find it in the morning."

Ella wrapped a piece of bright orange cloth round a twig and moved further along the slope, following the director. "Do you think we might get one?"

"One what?"

"A yeti."

Ana pushed a strand of long dark hair behind her ear. She thought for a moment and then shook her head. "At first when we started these expeditions, I thought maybe, just maybe, we might find something. Perhaps there was some truth to all the stories. But we've searched the south face of Everest, trekked across the high plateau of Tibet, got lost in the Karakorum ranges – and not a hair. I'm

6

sorry to say that it's likely to be the same here."

"But it *could* be different," said Ella.

Ana shrugged. "I'm afraid even the studio has pretty much given up. They've cut the programme's budget to pieces. We used to have a full crew, but now there's just the three of us – and you, of course," she added. "I don't mean to throw cold water on the trip. There's just part of me that wishes we could go back to filming real wildlife, instead of chasing shadows."

"But maybe you only see shadows because yeti are good at hiding," said Ella.

Ana laughed. "Yes, I suppose you're right. If I was a yeti, I'd avoid humans like the plague."

"Last camera," said Ella, handing it over.

They moved close to the rocky ledge. Ella watched the director biting her bottom lip in concentration as she worked, one eyebrow arched. Ana finished securing the camera, and switched it on, watching for the little light. "OK, that's all done. The trap is set!"

The daylight had all but deserted them down in the gorge and, even though the sun was still gleaming on the high, snowy peaks, the woods had deepened to a dark purple. Ella shivered, zipping up her jacket as they went back to camp.

Ella liked the young director – the way Ana knew everything about all kinds of animals, the fact that she was so confident travelling deep into the mountains a long way from home. But Ella thought she might just be plain wrong about the yeti.

While dinner bubbled in the pot and the others chatted in low voices around the fire, Ella climbed into her tent and scrolled through some of her photo journal. She'd got pictures of monkeys, more monkeys, vultures soaring on invisible currents above their heads. And the yak – plenty of yak. And tomorrow maybe she'd add a photo of a yeti. How was she supposed to get any sleep tonight?

Ella put away her camera and reached for her torch and a book. There was a tap at her tent flap.

"Come in!"

The zip opened and Uncle Jack's head popped through the gap. "I thought I'd check to see if you were settled in OK."

"I'm fine, thanks." Ella flashed her torch round the tent. "I've got my bed all sorted and my clothes are laid out over there." She pointed to a tidy pile. "And those are my souvenirs." She waggled the torchlight over a small collection of pine cones, river rocks and moss.

"Looking good," said Jack. He spied the cover of the well-worn book in Ella's hands. "Hey – *My Family and Other Animals*. Gerald Durrell is a hero of mine – he taught me so much about nature. But what's with all the teeth marks on the cover? I love the book but not enough to eat it."

Ella laughed. "It's not that. At home, I like to read sitting up in trees, but I need two hands to climb." She put the book in her mouth and mimicked climbing.

"Got it," said Jack with a smile. "Dinner won't be too long. You need to get the plates and things ready."

"I'll be right out."

Hot dinner round a campfire with her famous uncle, mountains, monkeys and the chance of discovering the yeti. *Not too bad at all*, thought Ella, reaching for her shoes.

An odd thing about humans, thought Tick as he thrust his spade into the soil for the yumpteenth time that afternoon, was their smell. Or rather the fact they didn't have one. How was it possible to go through life without a smell?

Tick *(he with no time to waste)* stopped digging and gazed around at the fungusatory – the walls of the cavern towering high, its jagged ceiling dimly lit by fireflies. On the cavern floor around him, dozens of hefty yeti milled about in the gloom – digging up soil, spreading new spores, turning over compost heaps. Even in the murk, Tick could still make out the unease on their shaggy faces. Worry hung over the fungus farm like a rain cloud.

Word had it that a group of humans had set up their cocoons beside the river, not a thousand strides from the sett. Humans rarely came this far north, and their sudden arrival had sent everyone into a spin. Yeti knew to stay well clear of people, as sure as eating pine cones gave you wind – or at least that's what every yeti learned.

But Tick's mother must have known something different. When he was just a fledgling, she crossed paths with humans – in broad daylight – and never even tried to deny it. The elders swiftly banished her, and the weight of disgrace still hung around Tick's neck like a boulder. No one even uttered his mum's name any more. She had become *she of whom no one speaks*. The mother Tick remembered was good, and kind, and true. If she had been with humans, there must have been a good reason.

And now humans were right here on the mountain.

Just go and look at them, a little fly of an idea buzzed in his head. *Maybe you'll find answers?*

Tick swatted it away. He kneeled down and, with gentle fingers, harvested a handful of tiny fungi, lifting them out and placing them in his basket. With the basket now full, Tick got up and tied the handle to one of the vines dangling from the ceiling. He gave the vine a soft tug and watched as the basket rose to the tunnels above, to be collected by Scatterer Yeti and dispersed on the forest floor and beyond.

It was always the same in the fungusatory, thought Tick. Each yeti in their place, like ants in a nest, their movements steady and methodical – spreading fungi into the world. Just like it was in his father's time, and his father's before him. Tick tried to remember his father but it was hopeless – his dad had passed on before Tick had even learned to walk. What had he made of life down here? There had to be more to the world than growing and picking fungi.

"Hey, Tick," came a voice in his ear, breaking him from his thoughts. It was Plumm *(she sweet on the outside with hard centre)*. Plumm was on watering duty, lugging a bucket. "Did you hear the news – it's all over the farm – there are humans on the mountain!"

"I heard." Tick tried to sound unconcerned.

"Oh yeah, humans within striding distance and Tick isn't interested," Plumm teased. She put down her bucket and parted the soft fur on her cheeks and found a nit, popping it in her mouth. "What do you think they're up to?"

Tick shrugged. "I doubt it's good."

"Humaaaans, we have nooo smell…" Plumm moaned, raising her hands and reaching for his throat, her face twisted into a grimace.

Tick laughed, raising his hands too. "We waaaant to find your settttt!" he wailed.

A shout came from across the fungusatory. "You two, back to work!" It was Nagg *(he who pesters)*, the fungusatory elder. Tick could see him over by the waterwheel, talking to Dahl, Guardian of the Sett. They

12

were probably discussing the human situation.

Dahl *(he who smells the fiercest)* was taller and wider than any yeti in the fungusatory, with great shoulders, and arms like tree trunks. In one hand, he held the mighty Rumble Stick – the Guardian's staff, worn smooth by generations of hands. Dahl's neck was thick, and his mammoth head rose into a slight cone shape.

"Better hop to it," said Plumm, lifting her bucket.

Tick bent down and picked up his spade again, pausing at the sight of a large and rather poisonous-looking centipede burrowing back down into the soil. He grabbed hold and showed the wriggling bug to Plumm.

"Want half?"

Plumm shook her head as she wandered off. "All yours."

"Suit yourself," said Tick, munching.

The message soon got round the farm that Greatrex was having emergency speaks about the humans in the grub hall before the naming custom that evening. Greatrex the wise, keeper of the carvings, silverback of the sett *(he who knows most)*.

When the final horn sounded soon after, Tick dumped his tools and, when he couldn't find Plumm anywhere, he mumbled a quiet goodbye to some of the others, and padded out of the fungusatory and into the passageway.

The tunnel climbed to the upper part of the sett, Tick following the signs back towards the yeti dens, though he could have found his way blindfolded. He stopped in his den to wash his hands and face, gave himself a quick run-over with his flea comb and left straight away.

But, when he got to the grub hall, he saw that all the benches were already full. Every yeti in the sett was there, the cavern full of nervous murmuring. He spied Plumm waving at him from the far end of the cavern, her nut-brown eyes dancing with excitement.

"I saved you a spot," she mouthed. Tick went over and sat down, giving her shoulder a fond pat. His best friend was always looking out for him. Plumm was an orphan too – she knew what it felt like.

At the head of the cavern sat the elders: Greatrex, with Dahl ever present at his right hand, joined by Nagg and the others from the Council of Elders: Lintt, Slopp and Gruff. In front of them, resting on a bed of moss, were the precious slabs. As ancient as the mountains, as ancient as the world itself. Chiselled into the heavy rock blocks, in flowery, old-fashioned yeti script, were the yeti laws. These were the words and history that guided every yeti deed. Legend said the Earth Mother set the laws in stone in the time of darkness, and passed them down to each of her children. Tick learned to listen to the slabs almost before he'd had a chance to break his first wind.

Written in the carvings was the tale of how Earth Mother sent her children out into the world. They spoke of the yeti known as Almas who went north to the land of the high plateau. They were tall and mighty – their legs long, their fur as red as earth. To them fell the duty to protect snow mammals. To the west were the Barmanou, guardians of mountains and glaciers. Across wide oceans were the Bigfoot – carers of mangroves and wetlands – and the Mono Grande, keepers of the toads. In steamy jungles lived the Mande Barung, growers of medicinal plants, and the Orang Pendek with their long hair, the protectors of tigers and forests. They were all there, carved in stone – twenty setts, their tales written in the old writing.

But now there were only nineteen left and the story behind that was drummed into every youngling. How one of Earth Mother's children abandoned her slabs – the one called human. And now, many cycles later, she didn't even look like a yeti at all. Humans had lost most of their fur and they didn't have a smell beyond the mildest whiff. They had even forgotten how to tree-stride.

So why had Tick's mum tangled with them?

You need to find out, buzzed the idea fly.

"Stop pestering," answered Tick aloud.

"What did you say?" asked Plumm beside him.

"Nothing."

16

Dahl thumped the floor with his great staff just once and the hall fell silent. Silent apart from the constant growling and rumbling of dozens of yeti stomachs. Greatrex rose to his feet, his silver hair long and his face as dark as night itself. He touched his hand to his chest, and then to his head. The yeti stood as one and returned his greeting. Greatrex waited for the gathering to take their seats again. He rested his hands on the slabs as he spoke, as if gaining strength from their wisdom.

"Malodorous yeti, before the joyous naming custom begins, we must turn our thoughts to a serious matter." Greatrex peered over the gathered throng to make sure they were listening. "No doubt you've all caught wind of humans coming to the mountain. Dahl, with his own eyes, discovered them from a distance yestermoon." This brought a round of anxious burbling.

Greatrex silenced the crowd once more. "It is written that, long ago, people and yeti were one and the same. But not now. Humans want to hunt us down, find our setts and expose us to their world. Beware: *the toad does not come into sunlight without good reason.*"

There were anxious murmurs of agreement throughout the cavern at the silverback's words.

Greatrex raised his hand. "I'm putting the sett on the hush. The mountain is out of bounds. No tree-striding, no foraging, no rummaging, no mooching, no wandering –

not so much as a stroll. So it is written in the slabs. Hear me as I speak."

Again the cavern filled with grumbles.

Flabb *(he with stomach like boulder)* raised a long, hairy arm. "But what of our grub? What will we eat?" He patted his enormous bulk and there were worried noises from some of the others.

Greatrex raised his hand. "Rest easy. The kitchen assures me that even after tonight's feast we will have enough grub to last us more than a few moons." He nodded over at Nosh *(she who makes nibbles)* in her apron. "And tomorrow Dahl will lead a collecting team on a secret gathering trip. We shall draw stalks."

Greatrex held up a hollow tree stump filled with grass stalks. Each one was marked with the scent of a yeti in the sett.

"I hope it's not either of us," Plumm whispered but Tick's fingers drummed on his knee, over and over.

"*Pick me!*" they said. "*Pick me!*"

Greatrex shook the tree stump, rattling the stalks, and then drew out the first one.

Dahl ran it underneath his large, wide nostrils. "Dulle," he announced *(she with blank stare)*, followed by Gabb *(she who prattles)* and Itch *(he with skin complaint)*.

Dahl took the final stalk and breathed in. "Tick," he intoned at last.

Tick's head buzzed. *Now you can go and see the humans for yourself,* said the idea fly. *You know that's why you wanted to be chosen.*

You think I should? thought Tick.

"Let the naming custom begin!" Greatrex commanded, to loud cheers from the crowd.

Once the guard yeti had returned the slabs to the council chambers, helpers brought sacks full of green pine needles into the hall and placed them round the room.

At the front of the cavern stood a small yeti, her youngling coat barely sprouted, holding her parents' hands, her eyes fixed on the floor. Tick felt for her. He remembered just how jittery he'd been at his own naming.

There was a fanfare of yodelling as Retch *(he with upset tummy)* marched into the hall, his arms outstretched like wings, a piece of wood in one hand, a blindfold of moss around his eyes. "Greetings, sweet-smelling beasts!" Retch bellowed. "I implore you – begin the needling!"

At this, the yeti swarmed round the sacks of pine needles, grabbing handfuls of the sharp green leaves and hurling them at Retch. A green cloud filled the cavern as more and more needles flew through the air. They stuck to Retch's hair as they fell, covering his head, his arms and his chest until there wasn't a single bit of the yeti visible. A couple of eager younglings picked up a sack and poured the contents over his head.

Then Dahl thumped the cavern floor with his Rumble Stick again, and the commotion died down. Retch stood there, arms still outstretched, blanketed in green. He had become the green creature spoken of in the carvings – he was the Leaf Yeti. The bringer of names.

Tick saw the worried youngling cowering at the sight of him.

"Hail the Leaf Yeti," commanded Greatrex.

"Hail!" replied the cavern.

"I have the naming bark," announced the Leaf Yeti. He held the piece of wood above his head to great cheers. The youngling's mother came up to receive it.

"What says the bark?"

The mother read, "She who picks the best fruit."

The Leaf Yeti thought for a moment. "Come forth, youngling," he ordered. The small yeti shuffled forward. The Leaf Yeti placed his hand on her head. "From this moon forth you shall be known as Pluk, *she who picks the best fruit.*"

"Greetings, Pluk!" shouted Tick, Plumm and the others.

Now the cavern broke into great yodelling:

"*She has her own name, she has her own na-a-a-me!*
Pluk the yeti, she has her own name!"

Pluk gave an uncertain smile and waved at the crowd, while her parents accepted the congratulations of nearby well-wishers. There was applause all round as the Leaf Yeti took his seat at the head of the cavern.

"Yeti, without further delay, let us feast!" announced Greatrex.

3

The next morning, at first horn, Tick reported for duty at the boulder blocking the sett exit. The truth was he'd overdone it with the spicy beetles at the feast, and his stomach was still grouchy. Tick studied the others in the collecting team, and Dahl – who always seemed to be on his case. Dahl was what you'd call a serious yeti.

The Guardian clenched his massive jaw and banged his Rumble Stick, calling them to attention. The fur along his spine bristled. "Right, yeti, you might like to think this is just another amble in the woods looking for flowers, but with humans out there it's a risky business. As of now, you're in super-super-secret mode."

Tick grunted to himself. This was much better than being stuck underground, turning dirt.

"Not a snapping twig, not a rustle," Dahl continued. "We don't crack our knuckles. Nothing louder than a whisper passes your lips. Keep your eyes and nostrils open. We blend in with the trees as if we're trees ourselves. We don't go anywhere near the south face, and we definitely don't pass wind. Understand?" Tick nodded.

Dahl gave out his instructions. "Dulle, you take the gully and head towards Jagged Rock – find as many fowl eggs as you can. Gabb, you're at Grub Hill – Nosh wants a big sack of juicy wrigglers. Tick and Itch, you aim for the mulberry patch in Fir Tree Clearing – enough for everybody."

"And where will you be?" asked Tick.

"Where you least expect me, that's where."

Dahl gave the word, and the entrance guards heaved and pushed against the boulder, grunting and groaning. At last, they rolled it to the side. All of a sudden, a gust of fresh mountain air blew into the sett, carrying the sweet smell of trees. Tick breathed in – the scent helping to steady his nerves. Dahl stuck his head out from between the rocks and, making sure the coast was clear, he led the collecting team out on to the mountainside. Dahl gestured to the guards, who came out of the tunnel and moved some thick bushes into place to hide the entrance.

They were up on a ridge on the north face of the mountain, looking down at the sweep of the forest below. It was good to be outside, thought Tick as he gazed at the greenery blanketing the mountain. To feel the warmth of the sun on his fur, and hear the whistle of the birds. And down below on the other side of the mountain, on the south face, there were humans by the riverbank. Actual humans. Tick's stomach gave a little lurch.

"We meet back here before the sun reaches its peak," said Dahl. "And, when you're out there, remember: *when a mouth is closed, mosquitoes cannot enter.*" With a murmur of agreement, the collecting party slunk away into the forest.

"Come on, Tick," said Itch as he dropped off the ridge and headed down the slope.

Tick waved goodbye to the watchful Dahl leaning on his Rumble Stick, and turned downhill to follow his partner. The soft, leathery soles of Tick's feet met the earth as if they were greeting an old friend and he kept his gait steady, rolling – his arms swinging low as he bounded along the forest floor. Tick glided through the whispering trees, seeking out the shade cast by their trunks, stepping from shadow to shadow, not leaving behind so much as a bent twig or a twisted leaf. He was at one with the earth and the forest – tree-striding the way yeti were born to.

With steady striding, Itch and Tick soon reached Fir Tree Clearing and the thick tangle of mulberry trees. Even though the season had almost passed, there were still enough shiny dark fruit glistening in the sunshine to fill their bags.

The two yeti got to work, plucking the mulberries and putting them in the carry sacks slung over their shoulders. They worked facing each other, the way they had learned as younglings. Easier to watch their backs that way. It occurred to Tick that yeti were always watching their backs. Sometimes he wished they were bolder.

Once both yeti had filled their sacks, Itch started back for the trail. "I'm going up a bit," he said. "I know where there are plenty of crickets – big, fat crunchy ones!"

"You go ahead. I'm going to stay down here and pick a few more mulberries. I'll be there in a tick."

"In a tick! Very funny. Well, suit yourself. Just keep an eye on the sun." Itch pointed up at the sky. "Or Dahl will have your hide for a rug."

As soon as Itch was out of sight, Tick stopped pretending he was collecting berries. What luck! He'd been trying to work out all morning how to get away from his gathering partner. Tick swallowed hard, attempting to calm the thumping in his chest. He had a plan brewing. Tick waited for a moment, wondering if he still dared to try to get a closer look at the humans. He knew he shouldn't – it went against every word Greatrex had spoken just last night.

But Tick had to go to them. To find out why his mum had broken the rule of the slabs. What had she known about humans that he didn't? Maybe he could prove she'd been trying to do the right thing, then the elders might let her come back. Tick allowed himself to dream that perhaps he could even find her again and bring her home. That was what he wanted more than anything. And it was worth the risk.

Tick made up his mind. He left the clearing, taking the trail that led round the base of the mountain. If he was swift, he could tree-stride to the south face, where he knew there was a rocky ledge looking down on the river. He'd have a quick peek to see what was going on, then double back and scramble straight up the mountain to the boulder at the north entrance. He'd be back before anyone knew he'd gone.

Now that's a plan, buzzed the fly inside his head.

Tick lengthened his stride, dipping in and out of the shadows, darting from tree to tree as if each was an island – running as fast as he could. He covered a thousand strides in no time at all, making barely a sound as he went.

Soon the ground became dry and hard, the path rocky. Tick slowed down – he was close. Now he could see the bend in the river and, just below on the clearing by the riverbank, a sight that made his heart race. It was the cluster of human cocoons.

Reaching the rocky ledge, Tick leaped into the nearest bush, dropping down low and holding his breath. The wind was blowing in the right direction so his scent wouldn't carry – he made sure of that. But what would Dahl say if he knew Tick was here? Too late to think about that now. Gathering up his nerve, Tick pushed to the front of the bush, and peered out through the leaves.

What abnormal things the human cocoons were – flaming orange and bright blue, ruffling in the wind like the feathers of the rainbow bird. There were four of them, with the biggest one in the middle. A fire burned in a small pit, the smoke catching on the wind. Nearby there were flat, round things which Tick guessed were something to do with eating, and strange objects made out of a hard, shiny material. Several yak wandered the clearing, munching on grass.

Then the cocoons burst open and a pair of humans emerged. How strange they were! Tick could hear them grunting to each other in an odd tongue. They staggered over to the river's edge, stamping their feet, and kneeled down by the water and began splashing their faces and necks. Then the pair went and sat by the fire, shivering.

There was a rustle from one of the other cocoons, and another human emerged into the sunshine. It was a small female. Judging by her size, she was a youngling, no older than him. The girl had long brown head hair, curious wide eyes, and a tiny nose as small as a pebble. Tick inhaled – but he couldn't smell a thing.

The pebble-nose girl tripped her way over to the river's

edge. There Tick watched her pick up some river rocks and fling them into the water so that they made a plop as they disappeared. The girl managed to make one or two of them skip over the surface and crash into the riverbank just below Tick's bush. The girl followed where they had landed and her gaze drifted up the cliff. Her eyes stopped at the rocky ledge, and Tick pulled back into the bush, his heart throbbing.

He waited before peeking his face out again, watching as the girl wandered over to the yak. Now she seemed to be talking to them, and giving their noses a gentle rub. This human spoke yak? That was a surprise. Tick could tell the pebble-nose girl was special. The way she seemed to breathe the forest in, her kindness to the animals. He'd keep an eye on her.

After making sure she gave each yak a handful of weeds pulled from the slopes, Ella stopped and gave Shaan a scratch between his horns. Shaan was her favourite in their small herd. Jet-black, with a crest of white on his forehead, he was clearly the leader. *Just like Uncle Jack*, thought Ella.

There'd been a couple of times on the trek down here where she'd almost slipped on the loose rock, and had to reach out to Shaan beside her to stop from falling, his bulk warm and reassuring. There was something comforting about his smell too – like dried grass in the summer. Who'd have guessed?

Now Ella leaned in and whispered in Shaan's ear. "Thanks again for getting me here."

The yak gave a little toss of his head and carried on munching.

Ella went over to Ana and Walker by the fire and raised the lid on the blue enamel teapot that hung over the flames. Seeing a healthy puff of steam, she took a cloth and lifted it off, pouring everyone a cup. While she drank her tea, Ella listened to the birds in the trees. One in particular stood out, repeating its shrill squeaking call in bursts. *Peep-peep-peep*. Pause. *Peep-peep-peep*. Ana heard it too, and rummaged around in the backpack by her feet, pulling out a pair of binoculars and scanning the trees.

"There you are," she murmured, breaking into a smile. "Over there, Ella. Picking at the moss growing on that big branch."

Ella ran to her tent and got her camera, then zoomed in to where Ana had pointed. Ella caught a flash of amber tail feathers bobbing up and down along the branch. The bird – a bit like a pheasant – had bright shimmering blue plumage on its wings and a little bobble on its head.

"Wow, it's like a rainbow. What kind of bird is that?"

"A Himalayan monal. Beautiful, isn't he?"

Ella's camera whirred.

There was a rustle from the tent behind them, and Jack came out, running a brush through his hair. He was wearing long black boots and camo gear, with a utility belt that jangled as he walked. He stood there for a moment, his legs planted wide, hands resting on his hips.

"Morning, Uncle Jack. There's a monal in the trees," said Ella.

"Tell me about it," Jack grumbled. "I was munched all night. And that's after I covered myself in insect repellent."

"Stop pulling my leg! You know the monal is a bird," Ella chuckled, showing him the image on her camera screen.

"Oh, *that* monal," said Jack, glancing at the photograph briefly. He turned to Walker. "Ready to film those establishing scenes?"

"I'm on it, Jack."

"Then a close-up of me waking up in the morning – a little bit of me talking to camera, then hand-held tracking of me going bush on the trail of the beast. Sound good?"

Ella sighed and switched off her camera. She could see Uncle Jack was busy. But, as Walker set up his gear, Ella felt her heart lift. *Filming! They were filming!*

Soon after, on the edge of the forest and out of sight of the tents, Walker was ready behind the camera. Jack appeared from the trees, his long hair tousled, his face streaked with mud.

"It's just after daybreak," he whispered, "and I've spent yet another night in the bush, with just a few flimsy branches and a handful of moss for a bed. My only companion, the Himalayan monal and its delightful song." Jack rummaged around in his backpack and pulled out what looked like a piece of bark. "This dried goat jerky is the only thing I have to look forward to for breakfast today. But no time to whinge. It's part and parcel of being Jack Stern ... yeti hunter."

Jack gripped the goat meat between his teeth and began gnawing. He just about managed to tear off a chunk and his face warped and twisted as he chewed.

"That's a wrap," said Ana finally.

"Yaargh!" Jack spat the goat meat on to the ground. "I told you to stop as soon as I put that meat to my lips!" He glared at Ana and took a swig of water from the bottle on his belt. "All right," he hissed. "Next shot. I'm talking to camera when I hear a noise in the trees. I give chase with you close by. Got it?"

"Got it," said Walker.

"Ella, can you throw a stone off camera?" said Jack. "Make it a big stone, with a big crash. We want a good sense of danger."

Ella frowned. "Really?"

"Just a little artistic licence. All part of the show," said Jack.

★

Up in his bush, Tick couldn't stop staring. These humans were the strangest things he'd ever seen. Even weirder than the giant toadstool with red spots he'd once found growing in the cesspit, which exploded into an incredible mess when he touched it. Thinking of the toadstool made Tick's stomach growl. He reached into his bag and took a handful of mulberries, nibbling as he watched.

Tick had no idea what the humans were doing – what the black thing was that one of them had perched on his shoulder like a vulture, or why the human silverback was playing hiding games. Tick could tell he was the silverback. The long, silver, shiny hair – much more magnificent than the others – the way he thrust out his chest, had the largest cocoon, and ordered the others about. Tick didn't care for the way he bellowed at one of the yak when it grazed too close to their cocoons. Clearly, he and the pebble-nose girl were different kinds of human.

Then, from behind Tick's head, there was a rustle in the leaves. Before he could turn, thick fingers wrapped themselves round his throat and took hold, and another hand clamped over his mouth. Tick's heart pounded; the hair along his back stood up. The strong hands stayed firm and he could feel fingers boring into the back of his head.

"Don't move!"

Tick froze, his toes clenching the ground. There was

only one yeti with a voice like that.

"Foolish yeti." Tick could feel Dahl's scorching breath and picture his lip curled in a sneer, yellow fangs bared. "Have they seen you?" Dahl's voice was no louder than a whisper of breeze.

Tick shook his head. He could still see the humans playing their game – the girl had picked up a river rock.

Dahl's hands relaxed a little. "Lucky for you. Now I'm going to let go and we are going to creep away without a sound. Then we're going to take to the path and go far into the forest. We are not going to look back."

Dahl let go. Stepping backwards, Tick slid out of the bush and up the mountainside, finding the shadows of the forest. He turned to face the Guardian of the Sett.

Dahl didn't say a word. The clamped jaw, the widening nostrils, the shining wildness of his eyes said it all. Dahl raised a thick finger to his lips, picked up his Rumble Stick, and then glided through the trees, making no more sound than a butterfly's wings.

Tick hung his head and followed close behind. As they hurried along, a black shape attached to a tree on the side of the path buzzed and clicked.

They slipped through the trees – Dahl was running now, his stride doubled in length – heading towards Jackal Canyon. Tick guessed Dahl would wait to make sure they were truly alone, then double back to the west and take the long path to the sett. Then Dahl would bring him to Greatrex and the Council.

Tick felt ill. He knew well enough what they would do. There was only one punishment for getting this close to humans and it was written in stone. Tick held back his tears and tried to keep up with the Guardian who leaped through the forest ahead of him as nimble as an antelope. Dahl was right: he was a foolish, foolish yeti.

"I'm sorry, Dahl," Tick whispered. "Dahl, I'm sorry." But the Guardian didn't hear.

Dahl slowed his pace as they approached the opening to Jackal Canyon, and climbed down into a hollow surrounded by thick greenery. Dahl knew the mountain better than most – he seemed to know where each boulder lay, every fallen tree. Tick was grateful they'd stopped. His legs burned.

Dahl still hadn't spoken a word to Tick, hadn't even bothered to look at him. Now Dahl grunted and pointed to Tick's mulberry sack. Tick opened it for him and the big yeti scooped out a handful, popping the berries into his mouth one by one, sighing as he did so.

"You know what the Council will say, don't you?" Dahl muttered across the hollow.

"Does the Council even have to find out?" As soon as he'd spoken, Tick wished he could pull the words back into his mouth.

Dahl's face wrinkled in disgust. "I am the Guardian, holder of the Rumble Stick. If the Guardian doesn't speak the truth, then who can? I ask you."

"Sorry, I…"

"Of course I have to tell the elders, even if it sits uneasily with me," Dahl snapped. "If we are not true to ourselves, young yeti, then we are nothing."

Tick had done well to hold back the tears, but now they began to escape. He wiped at his eyes with the back of his hand and sat there, sniffling. If only Mum and Dad were still here.

"Why?" asked Dahl at last. "Why did you have to go to the river?"

Tick lifted his head. Though Dahl's face was still stony, the angry sparkle in his eyes had softened.

"I needed to find out."

"Find out what?"

"Why Mum did what she did all those years ago. She wouldn't have had contact with humans for no reason."

Dahl chewed his fruit. "Her banishment feels like a lifetime ago," he said at last. "Nothing good comes from mixing with humans."

"Then why did she?"

Dahl shook his head. "What was said in the Council chambers never reached my ears – I was not the Guardian then, and your mother couldn't bring herself to explain.

She may have made a bad choice, Tick, but your mum had a good heart, no matter what else you've heard." Dahl got to his feet. "Now we should be moving. We must get back to the sett before we find ourselves stuck out here on the mountain."

At the little camp by the river, the shoot came to a close. Ella darted about the clearing, helping Walker and Ana pack up their gear. She enjoyed being behind the scenes, watching how it all worked. Walker even let her peer through the lens a few times – it looked a whole lot different from how it did on TV.

"Can we go and check the camera traps?" Ella suggested. She'd been itching to look all morning.

Ana smiled. "I was going to have a cup of tea but seeing as you're so keen…"

Ella and Ana waded through the gurgling river and began looking for the cloth markers tied to the trees on the other side. At the first one, Ana crouched down and undid the clasp, taking out the camera. A quick scroll through the menu showed it hadn't filmed anything. Ana restarted the camera and put it back in the box.

They moved on to the next one. The file showed a long, slinky shape caught in infrared, bobbing in front of the lens, with a dark face and bright chest. The creature clambered on the tree trunk, shoving its nose all over the camera lens.

"We've got something!" gasped Ella.

"Look at that! A yellow-throated marten – pretty, isn't she?" Ana pressed save and put the camera back. "Why don't you check the one we put near the ledge, and I'll finish down here?"

Ella climbed further up the ridge and found the marker. She opened the black box, lifted the camera and ran the file.

Then she almost dropped it.

It was the shock of it. Her entire body felt cold. Ella pressed play again, and then again. Each time, her eyes widened a little more, her mouth became a little drier. Big hairy creatures rushing past the camera. Two of them – much bigger than humans – running on two legs, swinging long, thick arms. The way they moved was so smooth, so effortless. A bouncing gait that seemed to make them flow through the woods. Ella heard the blood thumping in her head. "Ana! Come quick!"

Ana left her camera where it was and pushed her way along the ridge. "Something interesting?"

"Uh-huh." Ella gulped, pressing play on the camera.

Ana's mouth hung open. "What on earth?" She watched the file again, her eyes searching. "A bear? Some kind of primate?" she stammered at last.

But Ella knew the creatures were no animal she'd ever seen before. One of them held a staff and the other carried what looked like a kind of bag. Ella hardly dared speak the words. "Are they yeti?"

"We must think like scientists," Ana insisted, replaying the video. "Study the evidence rather than jump to conclusions."

But Ella wasn't watching the video any more. She got to her feet and looked into the forest. These were daylight images. What if they were still here, watching? She turned this way and that, eyes scanning the mountainside. She couldn't see anything but there was a smell. A real stench. Like a barnyard that hadn't been cleaned in ages.

★

Tick watched as Dahl looked deep into the woodland. The Guardian listened for a moment, and seemed satisfied that they were alone, then he climbed up and out of the hollow and coasted into the trees without a sound, heading towards the grey scab of rocks that cut through the forest below them.

Tick had rarely come near Jackal Canyon – yeti avoided the place if they could and, in return, the jackals stayed clear of the sett. Jackals hunted in pairs, drifting through the forest, trailing anything that happened to cross their path – fledgling birds, helpless deer, trembling rats. *"Beware the lone jackal,"* went the saying, *"or the bite of its partner your backside will feel."*

Seldom did yeti ever fall prey to jackals. It had never happened in Tick's lifetime, but every youngling knew by heart the tale of Rashe *(he with no thought)* who chose to ignore his mother's words and went foraging near the canyon at dusk. Legend said his bones still lay about the rocks, bleached white by the sun. "You don't want to end up like young Rashe, now do you?" many a parent threatened at dinnertime. "Eat up your slime and stop complaining."

He was safe as long as he was with Dahl, thought Tick as they reached the head of the canyon. No jackal in his right mind would dare take on the Guardian. A swing from the Rumble Stick and it would be over before it started. But, as they dropped down between the boulders, Tick spied a scattering of bones, like white twigs.

The dusty path took them down into the shadows, where rock walls rose up on either side of them like a pair of giant jaws. Tick glanced from side to side, all the while keeping an eye on Dahl's hairy back. He imagined he could see the glint of eyes in the dark hollows between the rocks. Even though a cold, harsh trial in front of the Council of Elders was all he had awaiting him back at the sett, Tick wanted out of the canyon as quick as his leathery feet could carry him.

It was only when they'd reached the end of the canyon and were almost in the welcome arms of the trees ahead that the jackals chose to emerge, guarding the boulders on either side of the path. A pack of them, their fur brown like river sand.

Dahl slowed his pace to a walk. Holding the Rumble Stick in both hands, he twirled it a few times so it cut through the air, just enough to make sure the jackals had seen it. Then, standing still, he lowered the staff to his side.

"Don't move. I'll handle this," he mumbled.

The jackals parted to make way for a lone jackal the colour of gold, the fur on his muzzle flecked with grey – the alpha, assumed Tick. The jackal gazed down for a moment, eyeing up the yeti, before leaping down from one rock to another. Then he stood on the path, facing Dahl, back arched, with a jackal guard on either side. If he was the least bit troubled by the sight of the Rumble Stick in the hands of a giant yeti, it didn't show.

Now the alpha lifted his muzzle to the skies, letting out a long, low series of whines, punctuated here and there with the occasional high-pitched bark. Tick listened as the alpha growled about the peace of their canyon being broken, of unwelcome intruders, of the ill will between yeti and jackal. Tick watched Dahl's face for any sign of movement, but the Guardian stood as still as if he was carved out of the stone of the canyon itself.

Finally, when the jackal finished, Dahl cleared his throat.

"I am Dahl, Guardian of the Sett, holder of the Rumble Stick, he who smells the fiercest." Dahl's words echoed down the canyon. "We mean you no quarrel. Human folk have come to the mountain, blocking our way home. It is for this that we have sought passage through your territory and disturbed your sleep. I ask that you let us pass, noble alpha, and we shall not look back, nor leave any sign that we have passed by. Hear me as I speak."

The hairs on Tick's back began to bristle and his nostrils twitched in warning. Something wasn't right. He turned his head just in time to see four more jackals emerge on the path behind them.

"Dahl," Tick hissed. But Dahl just raised his hand, keeping his eyes on the alpha.

The jackal pack stood there for what felt to Tick like a lifetime. At last, the golden jackal bared his teeth in a terrible grin and seemed to chuckle. He gave a nod of his head in the direction of the others and the pack stepped backwards, away from the path.

"Come," Dahl gestured to Tick.

But, as Dahl took a step forward and made to leave, the alpha jackal raised his leg in the air, arcing a stream of pee across the path – the stinking liquid almost catching Dahl on his foot.

Dahl froze, eyes glaring, and Tick could hear the Guardian's teeth grinding, the bones in his back cracking as he tensed with fury. One by one, the other jackals cocked their legs, until the soil on the path was streaked and damp.

Dahl growled and let out a long, hot breath – Tick could almost taste the anger riding on it. Tick could tell Dahl was making a choice. Fight or walk. Then the Guardian nodded at the alpha, carefully stepped over the damp patch and carried on walking. Tick followed close behind.

Even when they were deep in the trees – back in the safety of the forest – they could still hear the yapping laughter of the jackals carried on the breeze.

6

On the other side of the mountain, in the safety of Jack's tent, Ella ejected the memory card from the camera and gave it to Ana, who pushed it into the laptop. Apart from the hum of the computer, there was silence.

The little ball spun in the middle of the screen and then, at last, a folder opened up. Ella prodded at the touchpad and the video began. They all leaned forward. Ella's heart was beating so loudly she was sure the others could hear it.

Finally Jack burst out, "Yeti! They're yeti!"

"This is huge," said Walker, stroking his beard.

"I still can't believe we actually found something," Ana murmured.

Jack crowed. "I knew I was on the right track! All those months of searching have paid off. All those expeditions. Finally this is proof!"

"Hold on now," said Ana. "I don't want us to be too swift in ruling out a species of undiscovered bear, which in itself would be fascinating."

"But what about the bag and the stick?" said Ella.

Jack snorted. "Come on, Ana."

Ana shook her head. "I still think we're reaching premature conclusions. Let's get some more experts to weigh in on this. We should try to upload it to the studio server back home."

"No way!" Jack spluttered. "This needs handling carefully. Who knows what might happen to the clip? Someone might break the news while we're stuck out here in the wilderness, and then what? No, Ana, I … *we* must be the ones to reveal the discovery. "

Ella saw her 'Girl Finds Yeti' headline vanishing.

"What do you suggest?" asked Ana.

"OK, you want more evidence? More evidence that this really is yeti we're dealing with? Fair enough – we'll get some. But we'll need tracking dogs and more equipment. I'll call up with our GPS coordinates and get a chopper to drop in right away."

"Good call, Jack," said Walker. "Whatever those creatures are, they would certainly have left a scent."

"I did smell something in the woods," Ella agreed.

Jack got up and paced the tent. "It's too late in the day to set off now, I reckon. We'll go as soon as we have the dogs. But we keep this to ourselves until I say so. No sat link, no messaging, no sharing photos, no getting in touch with the studio. Total blackout, got it?" ordered Jack. "We've made the most sensational find of the century, and I want to milk it."

"No worries," said Walker, getting to his feet.

"Sure, Jack," said Ana, following the cameraman out of the tent.

With the others gone, Jack and Ella watched the camera clip one last time. Then Jack closed the laptop and grinned. "I can't tell you how great this makes me feel, Ella. I'm going to be the first person in history to prove yeti exist. No one believed I would!"

"I did," said Ella.

"It's a shame old Ray Stevens isn't around to see it – our discovery would have cleared his name." Jack sighed, shaking his head. He went quiet for a moment, then his face brightened. "Never mind, the secret of the yeti will soon be out. This series is going to be massive, Ella. Week after week, the whole planet will be glued to their screens. No more hiding in the forest any longer for our hairy friends." He reached into his rucksack and took out the satphone. "Now off you go. I need to call in the chopper."

Ella had a question for Uncle Jack on the tip of her

tongue. A niggling doubt about the TV show and the yeti. But Jack started dialling, so she ducked out of the tent. Now wasn't the time.

★

When they were inside the mountain with the boulder rolled back in place, Tick slumped against the wall of the tunnel, his legs weak and unsteady. A haze of worry and guilt wafted from his body. Now it was the turn of the other members of the collecting party to grumble and complain.

"Thanks a lot, Tick," Itch complained, scratching himself. "We were out there for hours on super-secret hush! And me with a rash as itchy as a log full of ants – have you any idea?"

Tick stared at the floor.

"Itch, go along and take the food to Nosh. Ask that she prepare you a snack – you've earned it. Tick, report to the Council chambers and wait for me there," instructed Dahl.

Tick handed Itch his collecting bag, stained purple with mulberry juice, and then slunk off down the tunnel, keeping his eyes down. The other yeti were just knocking off work, and it was rush hour. Hardly anyone looked up as he passed. In some dens, pairs of yeti hunched over game boards, scooping up stones from the hollows and scattering them.

In the games hall, a group were flonking dwiles: swinging dirty, sopping rags through the air, connecting with the occasional splotch as they slapped a face. As he passed the library, Tick was pleased to see everyone was too busy reading to look up. He hurried along, hoping more than anything that he wouldn't bump into Plumm. He wasn't sure he could face her just yet.

Tick followed the signs to the Council chambers without so much as a word to anyone. He'd never been in front of the Council before. The chambers sat there, empty and grim. Tree stumps worn smooth from the backsides of many elders circled the giant stone meeting bench. Tick waited just inside the doorway, his stomach gurgling with worry. He had a sudden image of Mum doing the same.

In the corner of the chambers, on a wide shelf carved into the cavern wall, sat the carvings, wrapped in their coverings – a lantern full of glow-worms flickering on either side. The slabs that he'd ignored. And, if Dahl hadn't come and dragged him away, he might have led humans to the sett door himself. Tick whimpered. Foolish, foolish yeti.

You were looking for the truth, said the fly inside his head.

"Go away," Tick snapped.

Now came the *tap-tap-tap* of wood on floor as the elders began to arrive. Tick wiped his eyes and hurried back outside the door.

The elders marched past Tick, their faces stern.

"Wait outside till you are called, youngling," ordered Nagg. He pulled the moss curtain over the doorway. While they waited for Greatrex, the elders shared their thoughts in angry whispers. Tick put his ear as close to the curtain as he dared – he could pick out each of their voices. He'd heard them enough times at sett meetings.

"Is it true?" asked Lintt *(she like a ball of fluff)*.

"We must hear from the youngling," answered Slopp *(he fond of mud)*. "But I fear he will just confirm the worst – Dahl saw the foolish mop with his own eyes."

This brought much muttering. "Flouting an uttering from the silverback himself. The shame of it all," Nagg snarled. "I can't say I'm surprised – that youngling is always late for work."

"Taking no notice of what was said," said Gruff *(she*

with rough voice).

"The whole sett has been put in danger," agreed Slopp. "Believing humans can be trusted – just like his mother before him."

Gruff snorted. "Who would have thought?"

"You know what they say: *the dropping never falls far from the pigeon*," said Lintt.

"Very true," agreed Nagg.

From further down the tunnel came the sound of another stick tapping. Tick pulled back. Now his legs really began to shiver. He fixed his gaze on his toenails, just visible at the end of his hairy feet. Soon his feet were joined by four others on the ground in front of him. Big feet – powerful feet. They stopped, and Tick looked up.

Tick had never seen Greatrex looking so wounded, so hurt. He was expecting anger, but this was far worse.

"You'd better come inside," the silverback murmured.

Beside him, Tick saw that Dahl was also downcast.

Greatrex pushed aside the moss curtain, and took his place at the head of the great stone meeting bench. He touched his hand to his chest, and then to his head, the Council Elders returning the salute, bringing their muttering to an end. The elders found their tree stumps, settling themselves around their leader, who gestured with a trembling hand in the direction of the slabs. Lintt and Slopp went to the carvings and unwrapped them, then, taking hold on either side, lifted them up and carried them over.

Tick stood at the end of the Council chamber, doing his best to keep his nerve. The idea fly went round and round in circles in his head until his brain hurt, but, no matter how hard he tried, he could find no wiggle room at all, no way out of this mess.

"Let us begin," said Greatrex. "Tick, you are brought in front of this Council to answer accusations most grave indeed. Our Guardian informs us that you took it upon yourself to go to the south face to spy on the humans. He found you in a bush not ten strides from them, peering down on the people as if they were a youngling's playthings. Is this true?"

Tick found just enough voice to utter, "Yes, it's true, O Greatrex."

This brought a round of fresh grumbling from the elders. "You knew better!" Greatrex snapped, his nose twitching as the scent of Tick's fear filled the room.

Tick tried his hardest to keep the tears back from his eyes. But now down they came, like a stream. "I wanted to find out. About humans. I wanted to show Mum hadn't done wrong," he sobbed at last.

"Foolishness," scoffed Lintt.

Nagg shook his finger. "Your mother admitted the crime herself. This very group of elders passed judgement on her."

"But she must have had a good reason to go to the humans. Surely she gave you a reason!" Tick wept.

"You dare to question us?" Nagg growled.

Tick shook his head.

Greatrex called for order. "Elders, we are straying from the matter in hand." He cleared his throat and studied the writing on the slabs. "Tick, you are hereby charged with breaking a direct silverback command. You are charged with neglecting your duties while on a super-secret gathering mission." Greatrex's voice rose to fill the cavern. "You are charged with placing the sett and every yeti in it in danger, and risking the very survival of our way of life. You are charged with consorting with humans. To these charges, how do you plead?"

Tick forced a lump the size of a river rock down his throat. "Guilty."

Greatrex looked round the room. "Then this matter is settled. I think you all know as well as I do that the laws are clear on the matter of punishment."

Now Dahl spoke up for the first time. "I must be truthful. This does not sit easily with me. Is there no way we can bend the rules a little in this case? Show some compassion?"

Tick lifted his head. This was Dahl?

"Impossible! The rules are set in stone," answered Nagg.

"Passed down from the times of darkness," said Slopp.

Nagg thumped the table. "We owe our very existence to the wisdom of the slabs. In these times of trouble, tradition must be our guide."

"Hear! hear!" agreed Gruff.

"But he's just a youngling," said Dahl.

Lintt folded her arms and turned her gaze away from Dahl. "Age has nothing to do with it."

Nagg turned to their leader. "O Greatrex, I find Dahl's attitude surprising for the holder of the Rumble Stick. It's the very decline of the ancient ways that has allowed the Collective itself to wither over time. Surely he must see that?"

Greatrex took Dahl by the shoulder. "This does not rest well with any of us, but they are right. We must stay true to the carvings. He has to be punished."

Dahl nodded, avoiding Tick's eyes. "As you wish."

Greatrex turned to Tick, his eyes filled with tears. "Guilty yeti, by the next sunrise you shall leave this sett and stride off into the world. You will stride for thirty moons and thirty suns. You will not look back, nor ever attempt to return or make contact. Furthermore, your name shall henceforth be Tick, *the senseless*, so that any who utter it can remember your foolishness."

Tick hung his head. Now every fledgling would learn his sorry tale just like that of Rashe, eaten by jackals.

★

Once Greatrex informed the sett of his crime, every yeti grew an ice-cold shoulder. In the end, it was only Plumm who came to say goodbye.

"Wow, Tick," Plumm croaked. She sat down on the edge of his nest, her bottom lip trembling. "Did you really do it?"

For a moment or two, Tick pretended to pick fleas out of his fur so he wouldn't have to look up. "When I was out there, Plumm, by the mulberry bush, I—"

"You weren't thinking is what."

"But that's just it, Plumm. I *was* thinking. About humans. Are they really all bad? I know Mum must have seen something in them. I needed to know she didn't risk our life together for nothing."

"So what did you see?"

"I wasn't there long enough to find out. But there was a human girl who seemed kind. That was something…" Tick's voice trailed off.

"Where will you go?"

"I suppose I'll go south. Find myself a cave somewhere." Tick's voice began to crack.

Plumm reached over and took his hand in hers. "Well, if I ever find myself there, I'll be sure to drop in."

"Does that mean you forgive me?" Tick asked.

"Someone has to," said Plumm, her voice quavering. "I'll miss you, Tick."

"Me too, Plumm," said Tick.

Plumm gave him a quick hug and, without looking back, she closed the door behind her. Seeing her go made Tick's heart drop down to his shaggy belly, leaving an aching hole in his chest. He started gathering up his belongings, putting them into his woven sack, his thoughts dark. In truth, there wasn't much to pack. He decided he wouldn't bother with any of it.

Tick caught his reflection in the water of the washing pool in the corner of the den. The broad ridge that ran across his forehead; the hair, thick and dark; the tiny eyes a bit too close together; the flared nostrils. He held his own gaze a little bit longer. There was no hiding the guilt. His foolish plan had almost endangered them all.

There was a heavy knock on the entrance. When Tick went to open it, the passageway was empty. But leaning against the doorway was a long wooden staff. It was a strong, solid-looking stick. Made smooth by lots of careful rubbing with sand. Just the sort of stick that would feel good in your hand if you found yourself striding down an unknown and lonely path.

Tick brought the staff to his nose and sniffed. The smell was unmistakable. This was Dahl's stick. It wasn't the Rumble Stick, of course, but it was Dahl's all the same. Now, through the darkness that clouded Tick's head, there was a little chink of light – like a glow-worm that had lost its way.

Tick made up his mind he wouldn't wait until dawn. After everything he'd done, he didn't deserve to stay, to call this place his home any longer. The entrance boulder lay closed for the night but he knew of another way out: the spreading tunnels. This maze of tunnels above the fungusatory was just big enough for a single Scatterer Yeti, on hands and knees, carrying a basket of fungus. Using those tunnels for anything other than spreading fungus was unheard of – but what did it matter? Soon Tick would be far enough away from the sett to be nothing but a bad memory.

Ella woke to the sound of thumping in the air. *The chopper!* She unzipped her sleeping bag and rolled out, already fully dressed, then strapped on her headlamp and pulled on her jacket. Clambering through the opening of her tent, Ella could see the helicopter hovering above the clearing, sending the yak into a frenzy of stamping. Searchlights bathed the forest in light and the rush of air from the beating blades rattled the sides of the tents.

Ana and Walker were already out, setting off signal flares to mark their location. Ella went to stand by Uncle Jack and watched as the pilot winched down a large crate, swaying in the draught. When it touched the ground, Walker unhooked the clip. Then, as quickly as it had arrived, the chopper roared away into the night.

Ella ran over to the crate. She could hear yapping and barking coming from inside. The tracking dogs! "Poor things! Let's get them out."

Ana and Walker undid the bolts at the end of the crate and lowered the flap. Inside, three dogs strained at their leashes, yapping and whining. Ella kneeled down and let the excited hounds climb all over her. They were small – hidden behind long, shaggy fur that reached all the way to the ground – some kind of mountain dog.

"Can they sleep in my tent?" asked Ella.

Jack shook his head. "They have a job to do. I don't want them distracted."

"Come on, we'll make them somewhere nice to sleep right next to your tent," suggested Ana.

She took hold of the leashes while Ella grabbed the blanket from the bottom of the crate. They shepherded the bouncing dogs towards the tents and tethered them to a rock. Ella gave them a pat each, and then went back to help unpack.

The crate also contained tins and boxes of food, mountain-climbing gear and a drone. But right at the back Ana found a rifle.

"What on earth are we supposed to do with this?" she said. "The only thing we shoot is a camera."

"Relax, it's just for protection." Jack took the rifle out of Ana's hands. "But, if a huge, aggressive monster charges at us, you'll be glad I brought it, that's all I'm saying."

Ana shook her head. "It's much more probable that the

creatures we filmed are gentle, reclusive herbivores. Think gorilla, orangutan. They're more likely to run a mile at the sight of us."

"You wanted us to get up close and personal with a yeti, Ana? You wanted more proof? Well, I'm going to get it. But my show, my way," Jack snapped. "We move out first thing."

"Fine, Jack, fine," sighed Ana, marching off.

"Whatever you say, Jack," said Walker.

As the others climbed back into their tents, Ella went over to pet the dogs again. For all the excitement, they seemed pretty relaxed, lying on their blanket next to each other. She ran her hands over their heads. "We don't like guns, do we?" she whispered. "No."

Uncle Jack had never used one on his shows before – not that she had seen.

High up on the mountain, Tick's furry feet quivered. He hadn't managed to get very far away from the sett when something caught his eye. A flying beast hovered in the air – many, many times bigger than even the largest of the birds found in the forest. This beast-bird made a terrific thumping unlike anything he'd ever heard before, a noise that roared over the mountainside like the worst kind of avalanche. Then the beast shot beams of fire from its belly, lighting up the forest, before rising up into the sky and flying off into the distance.

"The humans," hissed Tick. He strode as fast as he could to get a better view. Down by the river, they were moving around like beetles – each of them carrying a lantern. "What are they doing?" Tick whispered. Then came a gust of wind from the direction of the river and carried on it was a sound no yeti wanted to hear. Barking. Could it be jackals?

Tick inhaled, trying to pick up a scent. There were at least three of the beasts, maybe more – it was too hard to tell. He shuddered. The jackals from the canyon were one thing, thought Tick, but these ones belonged to the humans. They weren't here for fun. He scratched his head, eyes fixed on the dancing lights far below.

What do you think is going on? said the fly in his head.

Tick didn't know. But one thing was certain: he needed to warn the others.

Tick doubled back and strode towards the spreading tunnels. Guilt coated every hair on his body. As he ran, he tried to work it all out – the firebird, the jackals and the frantic activity down by the river. The humans must have seen him and jumped into action. And now they were on his trail, tracking down the sett. The way humans always did, according to Greatrex. But he'd been so careful down by the river. Hadn't he?

As Tick ran, he wept. Banishment from your home was one thing, but it was another thing entirely to bring the sett to ruin.

When he reached the boulder blocking the way back into the spreading tunnels, he pushed it to one side. Soon after, he was back in the Council chambers in front of the elders for the second time that moon. Hardly daring to raise his eyes off the ground, Tick relayed everything he'd seen.

"Sound the alarm and call emergency speaks immediately," said Greatrex when Tick had finished. Dahl disappeared down the dark tunnel. Shortly after, Tick heard the mournful howl of the warning horn blowing through the tunnels, jolting each yeti in the sett from their sleep.

"To the grub hall," commanded Greatrex. "You too," he said to Tick.

When all the panting and puffing yeti joined Tick and the elders in the grub hall, rubbing their eyes, Greatrex rose to speak.

The silverback's voice rolled over the cavern like a wave. "You know what they say: *when you have figs in your haystack, everybody seeks your farm.*"

"True, true," some of the yeti mumbled.

"Fragrant-smelling brethren, we face a grave danger. We have learned that the humans by the river will soon be coming to seek out our sett. They may come as soon as sunlight allows." The cavern rumbled with anxious burbling and grumbling.

"It's that fool youngling's fault!" someone shouted out.

"He was seen, wasn't he? He really is senseless," came another voice.

"Hope it's you those humans get hold of, and not the rest of us," one of them spat.

Tick kept his eyes on the floor.

Dahl thumped the Rumble Stick and the noise faded away. Burpp *(he with sour belchings)* let rip, and now there rode on the air the most vulgar smell. Even in his distress, Tick paused to breathe in appreciatively.

"Apportioning blame does not help our cause." Greatrex threw his gaze over the cavern from end to end. "We must be strong, we must be watchful, but, above all, we must be calm." He paused. "It is time, dear friends, to abandon sett and seek higher ground. We travel to Staunch Veil."

Staunch Veil. Tick knew of only a handful of yeti who had ever been there. The Mountain Yeti stronghold, a cave so deep that it had no end. High in the mountains, close to the land of snows. Again the cavern filled with worried murmurs.

"And what of the fungus?" came a voice.

"I fear we must abandon our fungus spreading. We just have to hope the forest will make do," said Greatrex. "Perhaps we can soon return. But for now you must go back to your dens. Gather your most precious, and wait for the call. Hear me as I speak."

Tick searched for Plumm as the yeti filed out of the hall, his heart lifting for a moment when he caught sight of her. Plumm gave him a sorry smile before she was lost in the crowd.

Once the cavern was empty of all but the elders and Tick, Greatrex gave his orders to Dahl in short firm bursts.

"There is no time to draw stalks. We must make the necessary arrangements ourselves. Call Mapp and two others of her choice. They will guide us. Explain that our journey must use the waters of the river…"

"…to hide our scent," said Dahl.

Greatrex nodded. "We must leave before light comes. Let us hope the flying beast of the humans does not return to look for us. Have Nosh and her crew gather food for our journey. As much as we can carry."

"Plenty of supplies."

Greatrex grunted. "There is one last thing. The slabs. Should the sett fall…"

"I have already posted guards, oh, Greatrex," said Dahl.

"They have sworn to carry the slabs to Staunch Veil and will not let them out of their sight."

"It warms my heart to know you watch over us all, Dahl."

Dahl bowed. "What about the youngling?" He jerked his head in Tick's direction.

Greatrex weighed things up for a moment. He stared at Tick as if searching for an answer. "Bring him with us," he said at last. "Even exiles don't deserve to become fodder for humans. We'll decide his fate later."

Tick watched from the rear as a convoy of anxious yeti
gathered at the north entrance. At the head of the line
was Mapp *(she who knows the mountain like her hand)*,
with Greatrex and the other elders. Burpp hadn't let up
and the tunnel reeked.

Each yeti carried their gathering sack, filled with what
few things they possessed. Some fledglings, the ones
that knew something was wrong, buried their face in
the fur of their mothers' legs, while others ran round the
tunnels, giggling and calling out, excited by the prospect
of adventure.

Tick stood with Dahl and the slab bearers, who were
tying the precious blocks to two poles like a wounded yeti
on a stretcher.

Tick felt a tug at his elbow. It was Plumm. "Are you
going to be all right?"

Tick managed a weak smile. "I guess so. I'm not being kicked out just yet."

"You did well to come back and warn us all. Remember that."

Tick shook his head. "It doesn't feel good."

On Greatrex's command, the yeti began moving out of the tunnel and into the darkness. Tick knew they would strike out along the ridgeline towards the mountains in the north that rose up higher than the clouds.

"Off you go, youngling Plumm," instructed Dahl.

Tick watched as Plumm joined the procession, the pang in his chest growing as she blended in with the other hairy backs. Plumm was his only friend. And soon he would have to leave her too. Tick wished he could at least walk this trail with Plumm, her mischievous grin lifting his spirits.

"You stay right beside me," Dahl muttered, as if reading his thoughts.

Dahl ordered the bearers to lift the slabs, and with a groan they heaved the poles on to their shoulders. When the last of the yeti had left the sett, the slab bearers followed. Dahl and two guard yeti jammed the giant boulder at the main entrance in as tightly as possible, sealed it with earth and then covered the spot with bushes. The humans would have to work hard to get inside.

"Pick up the pace, yeti!" Dahl barked.

★

After a quick breakfast of fresh, hot camp bread and tea, Ella led the others across the river to the spot where the camera had caught the footage, the yapping dogs pulling her along. Was today the day they would find a yeti? Things were moving so fast. Beside her, Walker led Shaan, who carried the camera equipment on his back.

Ella stopped when she reached the tiny cloth flag tied to a branch.

"Ella, pull the dogs over and let them have a good sniff," commanded Jack. He was dressed head to toe in camo gear, the rifle slung over his shoulder. Ella thought he looked more as if he was on a big game safari than a wildlife programme. Underneath all the excitement, Ella felt a little twinge of doubt. Was this a documentary or a hunt?

The dogs began straining at their leashes. Noses twitching, they howled and circled the rocky ledge before looking towards the thick of the forest.

"I'll take over from here." Jack tucked his gun in Shaan's saddlebag and grabbed the leads from Ella. "Make sure you get plenty of shots of me handling the dogs, Walker."

★

The sun soon started its journey across the sky and Tick suspected it wouldn't take long for the humans' jackals to pick up their scent. The yeti needed to get to the river sooner rather than later.

Thinking of jackals brought the idea fly buzzing back into Tick's head.

What is it? grumbled Tick.

Why don't we go into Jackal Canyon?

What do you mean?

March straight in. Make the canyon stink of yeti scent. I mean really stink...

Tick's eyes lit up. *And trick the humans into searching the place!* The fly had something there. It might buy them a little more time. He called out. "Dahl, Dahl!"

"Yes," Dahl muttered, coming round from the other side of the slabs to face him.

Tick winced at the sight of Dahl's nostrils flaring as he told the older yeti his idea. He was likely to get a tap on the nut with the Rumble Stick for even suggesting such a thing.

Instead, Dahl called over a yeti guard. "Run up the line, as quick as you can, and pass this message on to Greatrex." The Guardian explained the plan.

"Jackal Canyon?"

"You heard me."

Dahl scowled at Tick. "Another one of your foolish ideas."

Tick waited until the Guardian couldn't see before

allowing himself a tiny smile.

Greatrex gave the word and, a short while later, Tick and the others trooped through Jackal Canyon. The bigger yeti walked on the outside of the line, shielding the fledglings who peeked out from gaps in the wall of hair.

The jackal pack sprang out from their dens, certain they were under attack. Tick gripped his staff as the alpha and his pack snarled and gnashed, the fur on their backs bristling with rage, but Tick ignored their threats – he knew they wouldn't dare strike. What could they do against such a force?

Dahl twirled his Rumble Stick through the air. He stopped for a moment and eyeballed the alpha as he passed. "Feel like cocking your leg this time?"

The alpha snarled and bared his fangs, but he didn't move from his rock.

Dahl chortled as he walked off. "I don't mind admitting that felt good." He beckoned to Mooch *(he who wanders aimlessly)* to join him. Tick overheard Dahl giving the yeti guard instructions to drop behind the convoy, hide in the forest and act as a scout – to keep him informed if the humans were still on their trail.

Tick hoped his Jackal Canyon plan worked.

★

The dogs led them through the forest until they reached a break in the trees. Ahead of them was a ravine, a channel of rock caught between a steep incline of loose shale on one side and the mountain on the other. Mist swirled above their heads. Ella stopped at the mouth of the canyon and peered in. Something about this place gave her the creeps.

"Interesting rock formations. Perhaps we should take a look," suggested Ana. "There could be some wildlife."

"Great idea. The canyon will provide some good shots," Jack said. "Let's tie up the yak here and take the dogs." He handed the leashes to Ella, then whipped out a brush from his utility belt and ran it through his hair. He hung the rifle over his shoulder.

"Do you really want the gun in the shot, Uncle Jack?" asked Ella, pointing. "As it's a wildlife programme…"

Jack thought for a moment, then took the rifle off his shoulder and put it back in Shaan's saddlebag. He grabbed the dog leads again and took up position.

"Action," said Ana.

"Rolling," said Walker.

Jack crept forward, eyes narrowed. He turned to the camera. "Our tracking dogs have led us here to this canyon and we're going to take a closer look. We might just see signs of a yeti. We've got to tread carefully. We don't want to…" Jack squelched into a pile of something wet and stopped. He stared down at his boot, wrinkling his nose. "Cut, cut." He scraped the sole of his boot against a rock. "What on earth?"

"It looks like poo," said Ella.

"Yeti?" gasped Jack.

Ana looked at the droppings. "Dog." She covered her smile with her hand.

Jack glared at the three dogs. "You mangy little monsters…"

They carried on into the ravine, the shaggy dogs frantically smelling their way from rock to rock. As they walked deeper into the gorge, the mist cleared for a moment, revealing a cave mouth higher up.

Ana spotted it too. "I'm going up for a closer look," she said, clambering up the slope, scattering loose shale down on to the ravine floor. She reached a rocky shelf and hauled herself on to it, flicking on her torch. Then a cloud of mist wafted in, blocking her from view. Walker tilted the camera towards her.

Jack guided Walker back to face him. "Catch my reactions," he whispered.

"What can you see, Ana?" Ella called up.

"Not sure yet." Suddenly Ana gave a shout. Through the mist, Ella saw her backing away from the mouth of the cave, feeling for the edge of the rocky outcrop with her feet.

Then, out of the fog, Ella saw a golden dog – more like a wolf – its muzzle flecked with silver, its fangs bared. By its side came two more, then from hollows in the gorge walls there emerged others.

Walker swung his camera. "Jackals."

"What should we do?" asked Ella.

"Don't look them in the eye," said Jack. "Just stand perfectly still. No sudden movements. Walker, camera on me."

All at once, Ana lost her footing and stumbled down the ravine, scattering rocks. At the sudden noise, the jackals leaped forward, growling.

"Run!" yelled Jack. He turned and began to race off, back in the direction they'd come from.

"Go!" Ana shrieked.

Ella sprinted as fast as she could, her camera swinging from side to side around her neck, not daring to look back, Walker by her side.

"Keep going!" she heard Ana shouting from close behind her.

They burst from the gorge and into the woods, darting between the trees until finally Jack came to a stop at the spot where they'd left Shaan. Ella leaned against a tree trunk, legs sore, chest heaving, the dogs panting at her feet.

Shaan looked at them, as if wondering what all the fuss was about.

"That's the last time I leave the gun behind," wheezed Jack.

While they all got their breath back, Walker checked his camera and fixed it once more to Shaan's saddlebag, and Jack fished out his black notebook and a large map. Ella peered over his shoulder. Even though Uncle Jack seemed to know what he was looking at, she couldn't make head or tail of it. Were they lost?

As she waited, Ella looked around. Long branches draped in moss hung over her head and above there was a covering of mist. She listened to the call of strange birds and the hum and click of insects. She adjusted the setting on her camera and took some photos, trying to capture the strange way everything looked through the cloud. Could they really find a yeti in this? The way she'd seen them move on the camera footage, she doubted they could ever catch up to them.

Finally Jack untied Shaan from the tree. He grabbed hold of the saddlebag and heaved himself up on to the yak's back. "Everyone ready? We keep heading north." With a whistle, he set off into the woods.

As the crew travelled higher and higher, the trees began to thin out. Ella was sure she could smell that rotten scent again. Out of the corner of her eye, she saw her uncle slip his rifle from the saddlebag and rest it over his lap.

At last, with steady striding, the yeti reached the banks of the river. Tick stared at the wild waters carving their way through the mountain. Ahead, the rock rose straight up from the river's edge like walls. The current was strong and Tick knew the water would be ice-cold too, coming from the ice melt of the Glacier of Aalf to the north.

He watched as Mooch, Dahl's scout, came drifting back through the trees. "They were delayed at Jackal Canyon, but the humans are back on our trail and gaining," he panted.

Greatrex conferred with Dahl and Mapp. "We will have to wade single file against the current, and quickly. We'll pick up the trail to the Veil on the other side when we can."

"The tunnels start a thousand strides or so past the bend," said Mapp.

"The fledglings and some of the others will struggle,"

Dahl remarked, staring at the torrent.

Greatrex sighed. "What choice do we have? To the waters!"

Mapp nodded and trudged into the river, feeling the rocks below with her feet. She was soon up to her hairy thighs, her teeth chattering.

Then Dahl gave the command, his voice rising above the roar of the river. "Advance!" he bellowed.

Tick tapped his staff uneasily as each yeti entered the river, grabbing hold of the one in front to make a chain, pulling as one against the current. Mapp strode ahead, showing the way, eventually vanishing from Tick's view round the bend in the gorge. The line of shaggy backs began to stretch upriver.

They might just pull this off, thought Tick. *Perhaps it won't be a total disaster after all.*

Now the last of the yeti stepped into the water – last but one. Plumm still lingered at the water's edge. She gave him a little wave and Tick couldn't help but smile.

"You coming?" Plumm mouthed.

"Right behind," Tick mouthed back, watching as his friend climbed down the bank and into the current.

"Slab bearers! Make sure those bindings are secure." Dahl turned to Mooch. "Hide yourself on the trail, a few hundred strides or so back. As soon as you see the humans approach, leave your post and hurry back here to warn us."

Tick gave a fearful glance at the woods. He wondered if the girl with the pebble nose was one of the humans on their trail.

"Let me go too, Dahl," he said quickly, before he had a chance to change his mind. "I can see if it's the same humans from by the river. I'm the only one that's seen them before. It may help us somehow."

Dahl thought for a moment. "Go – but take no chances. Hide well and come as soon as you catch sight of them. Don't delay."

"I won't," said Tick, running after the scout as he disappeared back into the forest.

★

The dogs were the first to sense a presence. Without warning, they jerked as one and broke free from Ella's grasp, tearing along the forest floor, yowling and chattering. Ella searched the trees, her breath catching in her chest. Then she saw it. A yeti.

Ella almost mistook it for a boulder, but then she glimpsed dark, unhappy eyes half hidden below a thick brow. Their glances met for an instant and in that moment Ella felt her entire body tingle.

Then the yeti bolted, a staff in its hands, and Ella saw there were two of them hurtling through the forest, moving at an astonishing speed.

"Th-th-th…" she stuttered. Then, "There!", jabbing a finger at the disappearing shapes.

Before Walker could grab his camera, Shaan was gone, bolting after the dogs – Jack bouncing along on his back. Yak and rider disappeared, Jack's shouts carrying on the wind.

"After him!" cried Ana.

Before they'd got very far, a rifle shot reverberated through the trees.

"No!" wheezed Ella. She raced ahead of the others and burst out on to the river's edge, trying to make sense of what she was seeing.

The dogs were barking at the water, Shaan's tether was caught in a branch, and Jack was gesturing upriver with a crazed spark in his eye. The rifle was lying on the riverbank and, to Ella's relief, there was no wounded animal in sight.

In fact, the total opposite. A huge hairy creature, very much alive, fought its way against the current, a pair of tree-trunk legs splashing through the raging water, arms flailing. Then it was gone. Ella climbed a nearby boulder and scanned the river, but the creature had vanished.

"I'm going after them!" Jack cried, running into the water. But it was clear that the current slamming against his legs was too strong.

Jack lifted his face and roared at the sky, then he

trudged back to the bank, his trousers soaked.

"Yeti – three … four, maybe more. They fled upriver," he said, when Ana and Walker finally appeared.

"I saw one too," said Ella. She pointed to the rifle lying on the ground. "You didn't shoot at it, did you?"

Jack shook his head. "The rifle went off when I dropped it." He sank down to the ground and put his head in his hands.

"Is there another way we can go upriver? Try to recover their trail?" asked Ana, peering.

"I don't think so," said Jack. "The rock on both sides is too steep."

"Then let's get that drone up, Walker!" said Ana.

They gathered round the screen as Walker piloted the drone, but after fifteen minutes of hovering, revealing nothing but river and mountain, Walker brought it back down.

Then, as they turned to leave, Ella spotted something downriver, caught against a rock. Two long branches lashed together with rope, in the middle of which was what looked to be an enormous bundle wrapped in cloth.

"Uncle Jack, look!" Ella called, pointing.

"It looks like some kind of stretcher," said Ana.

"Whatever it is, we need to go in and get it," said Jack. "It must belong to the yeti – it has to."

As she watched Ana and Walker brave the water, Ella

felt a sudden ache of remorse. The yeti had fled from them. They were scared. Whatever this bundle was that they'd just found, the yeti couldn't have meant to leave it behind. What had they done?

★

Tick watched the humans, his fists clenched, hoping they somehow wouldn't see the slabs caught in the water. Then Pebble Nose pointed to the river and Tick knew all was lost.

Back in the jungle, for an alarming moment, their glances had met. He'd never forget the look of surprise in the girl's eyes. He and Mooch had fled, striding like never before, until they reached the river and warned the others. The slab bearers had been forced to drop the carvings and run – Dahl had given them no choice. In his hurry, Tick had panicked and thrown himself out of sight behind a rock. Then the human silverback had burst out of the jungle on the back of a yak, and his thunderclap had roared and rumbled.

Now the other humans gathered. They waded into the water, battling the river with their stick legs. Once they reached the slabs, they took hold of the stretcher poles, but struggled to lift them. Pebble Nose and the silverback went to help, and somehow they dragged the stretcher on to dry land, where they collapsed on the ground. Tick buried his head in his hands. The slabs should have been at the head of the convoy, next to Greatrex.

Got any plans now? he whimpered. But the idea fly was nowhere. Tick calmed his breathing down, then poked his head back out as far as he dared. There was no sign of Dahl, Mooch or any of the others. Plumm was nowhere to be seen. When the thunderclap boomed, everyone had fled.

Tick searched for a way out of this predicament. What if he waded across the river and charged at them? But there were four humans, three jackals, a massive yak and the thunderclap against one of him. He'd have to find another way.

Tick watched as the humans undid a little bit of the covering and peered in. Touched the precious carvings with their human hands. They seemed pleased. Even creatures as foolish as humans could sense the importance of the slabs. The silverback strutted about like a rainbow bird. Then they wrapped up the slabs again and lifted the poles from one end, tying them to the back of the yak. *Clever*, thought Tick. The yak could drag the slabs down the hill.

Tick watched the humans disappear once more into the forest. They'd be heading back to their cocoons, he guessed. He decided he would go there too, so he could keep the slabs close by until he figured out what to do. He crept away from the river's edge and took to the trees. He would get to their camp before they did and lie in wait.

Tick drifted through the jungle, the leathery soles of his feet meeting the soil, his gait rolling and steady – arms swinging low, his fur blending in with the trees. Tick felt sick to his stomach. His fixation with clearing his mother's name had landed the sett in deep trouble. Of course humans would try to find them – that's what they did. Why had he thought differently? If he had listened to Greatrex, then none of this would have happened. And now the slabs were in human hands.

"Eat up your clay," Tick could hear mothers warning their children for moons to come. "Eat it all up unless you want to turn out like Tick the senseless."

He had to find a way of making it right.

The human camp by the water's edge showed no signs of the humans – Tick had arrived first. The skin of the cocoons fluttered like leaves in the breeze, the yak tethered further up the clearing snuffled as they grazed and the birds called, but other than that there was nothing. Tick breathed in. He caught the smell of burnt wood, of yak fur – warm from the sun – and jackal scent.

Perhaps you should do something to the cocoons! The idea fly buzzed into life. *What if the humans came* back and found everything ruined? They might get scared. They might decide to leave the slabs and run away.

Are you sure? Tick gulped. It was not in a yeti's nature to be destructive. It went against the yeti laws.

Desperate times call for some rule-breaking, the fly pointed out.

You're right, agreed Tick. He glanced around, making sure the humans weren't approaching, before wading across the river. *Time I repaid the humans for all the trouble they've caused.*

The yak caught the whiff of the young yeti and snorted at him as he passed, stamping their hooves.

"Don't mind me, just carry on with your dinner," Tick said, striding up to the first cocoon. It was easy enough to push over. He just snapped the thin sticks that held it up, and it collapsed in a heap. Tick took hold of the skin and dragged the whole thing into the river to give it a good dunking, before flinging it back on to the rocks with a *SPLOT* like the droppings of a goat with an upset stomach. He got started on the other cocoons, tearing them to shreds, before ripping a hole in the silverback's cocoon and going to work with his staff, smashing and stomping everything inside.

Tick spied a black, shiny thing. It was tucked underneath some coverings, hidden in the corner like a secret. A light on it blinked like a firefly that couldn't make up its mind. Tick threw it up in the air and let it hit the ground, smashing into several pieces, then gave it several thumps with his staff for good measure.

See how you like that, thought Tick.

The sun was already dropping behind the mountains by the time Ella and the others straggled back to camp. Ella's feet were tender, her knees like jelly, but none of that seemed to matter. As she stumbled along, she couldn't stop thinking about the yeti in the trees – the mournful look in its eyes.

It occurred to her that the creature hadn't been there by chance. It was as if it was keeping a lookout. *They were expecting us to come*, thought Ella, *and that means they're clever*. Before the film crew turned up, the yeti were at peace. And now they were on the run.

It made Ella think back to a summer a few years ago, when her family used to live in the countryside. Near her house there was a sheltered creek. Not everyone knew it was there – you had to push through the bush for a while, weaving through the trees until you came to the bank. It was like knowing a secret. Then, if you sat still for long enough, staring down at the lazy water, you could spot dark eels drifting out from the reeds, weaving against the flow like ribbons. Ella never got tired of watching them.

But one day a pair of boys from her school must have seen her entering the bush, and followed her trail. She turned and saw them stomping behind her through the undergrowth, whooping when they spotted the creek. Before Ella knew it, they had reached into their backpacks and pulled out hand lines and hooks.

She watched in fear as they fixed their bait and dropped the hooks into the water. Ella knew they weren't after the eels for food. These boys wanted to try and land them simply for sport – just because they could.

Ella wanted to explain that the eels were special. There weren't as many around as before. That, if conditions were right, they could live to be a hundred years old and that they deserved more than a grubby hook.

Ella wanted to tell them all of that, and more. But she just sat there, trembling. And when she couldn't take it any more – the thought of seeing them catch one was too much – she got to her feet and scrambled away, face burning. She knew it was all her fault. The boys only found the eels because of her.

Now as Ella walked through the forest, thousands of miles away from home, she hoped their film crew hadn't just done the same thing to the yeti. She'd dreamed of big yeti headlines but now Ella wasn't so sure she wanted that at all.

Uncle Jack caught up to her and patted the bundle they'd retrieved from the river. "Camera-trap footage. Real yeti objects. We've got them now, Ella!" He grinned. "What a trip this is turning out to be."

Ella didn't smile back. Uncle Jack was supposed to be the person who wanted to protect nature. Jack Stern, wildlife supporter. But now it was becoming clear to her that her uncle was after something completely different.

★

Ella and Shaan were the first to emerge from the forest to their campsite by the river. Ella gasped. The tents were flattened and equipment lay scattered about the clearing: sleeping bags, pots, pans, books, tripods, food – the lot.

"What the – the camp!" Jack hissed as the others caught up. He slipped the rifle off his shoulder.

"It's been ransacked," said Walker.

"Robbers?" said Ella.

"Not this far out, surely," Ana said, looking puzzled.

"Monkeys?" said Walker. "What about those jackals?"

Ana nodded. "You're right. Something came for our food."

Jack spotted his tent, still standing but torn to shreds. He let out a groan. "The laptop…"

"And the clip from the camera trap!" said Ella.

Walker rushed to the tent and then came back out, pieces of computer in his hands. "I think we've got a problem."

"Oh no…" Ana took the laptop from Walker and set it down on the ground. The case was completely crushed. She ejected the memory chip from the side, but, as it came out, it fell apart.

"We have a copy, right?" said Ella.

Ana shook her head. "We didn't upload it on the sat link. Not even on to an external hard drive."

"And I didn't get one shot of the creature today," said Walker.

"Why did we leave that chip here? Why?" Jack moaned.

"You still have those, Uncle Jack," said Ella, pointing to the bundle on the poles.

Jack nodded. "True. We need to have a proper look – right now."

Ana and Walker undid the ropes holding the poles and freed Shaan, who wandered over to the other yak to graze. Ella led the exhausted dogs over to their blanket and gave them a big bowl of food – somehow the dog biscuits hadn't been touched.

Then Ella and the film crew stood round the bundle, a little hesitant. Finally, Ana kneeled down and untied the covering, letting it fall to the sides. Jack put down his rifle and turned on his headlamp.

There were five slabs, each about the size of a coffee table. Little flourishes and curls, delicately carved into the rock, covered the grey stone blocks. The slabs looked old to Ella, the edges worn smooth as if by the touch of many hands. She ran her fingers over the stone, a quiver running up her arm.

"They're beautiful," she said at last. She wanted to take some photos, but then remembered Uncle Jack had said not to.

"Totally astonishing," Ana mumbled, her hands over her mouth. "It looks like script."

"Yeti can write? Wow," said Jack. "Didn't see that coming."

"I wonder what it says?" said Ella, tracing the writing with her fingers.

"We'll need to have it examined by a linguist to work that out – and find out who carved it. These things may yet be human," said Ana.

"Please, Ana. We saw the yeti running away. Then we found these things right in their path," said Jack.

"They have to be connected," agreed Walker.

A smile broke over Ana's face. Ella could see the director was starting to believe the slabs belonged to the yeti too. "This is mind-blowing," Ana chuckled.

Jack grinned. "I can see the teaser for *Yeti Quest* now." He got to his feet. "Mood lighting, dramatic music, a close-up shot as the camera tracks along the slabs. *Join Jack Stern as he discovers a secret as old as the mountains. Join him on the quest of a lifetime. Join him on a quest for yeti.* This is going to be the biggest show for years. Red carpet, awards, the whole deal." Jack laughed. "We'll do a lecture tour – that'll go viral too. There could be merchandise tie-ins, movie rights, you name it. Everyone everywhere will have their piece of yeti."

Ella felt her chest tighten. What if the yeti didn't want to be part of all that?

Jack leaned down and pulled the coverings back over the slabs. "But first we have to make sure these things are safe – get them into that packing crate and secured. Just in case the animals that did this to our camp come back. I'd better stand guard." He picked up his rifle again.

Ella looked round at her sopping tent. She went over and picked it up, and let it drop back down. Her sleeping bag was still in there too. She spied their food supplies, crushed and mangled. Her favourite book. "Where are we going to sleep tonight? What are we going to eat?"

"Well, let's get a big fire going, and then see if we can't

dry out our bags, and then try and patch together the last tent standing," suggested Ana.

"I'll see what food is salvageable," added Walker.

"I'm on the firewood," said Ella.

Back over by the trees, she stopped and peered into the forest. Then she bent down and started gathering twigs.

★

From his vantage point on the other side of the river, Tick couldn't stop a little smile of satisfaction taking hold. Ruining the camp had been a good idea. He could tell it was a complete shock to them – the way their shoulders dropped, the way they stumbled around, looking lost. The stunned expressions on their faces when they saw what he'd done to the shiny thing.

But, for all their worried looks, they weren't running away in fright as he'd hoped. In fact, they looked like they were setting everything back up as best they could. Pebble Nose was building another fire.

Then Tick froze. There was a smell on the wind – foul and potent. He knew that smell. But, before he could turn round, a massive hand clamped itself over his mouth and hot breath whistled in his ear like flames.

"Senseless yeti," came the hiss.

Tick swallowed.

"The camp of the humans – was that you?" said Dahl. Tick nodded.

"Dishonourable youngling. Since when does a yeti—" Dahl shook his head and lifted his hand off Tick's mouth. Tick could see he didn't have the strength to bother telling him off.

"I had a plan," whispered Tick. "I wanted the humans to get scared and run away, leaving the slabs behind."

"Doesn't seem to have worked, does it?" said Dahl.

Tick dropped his head, and let out a long sigh.

"Just as well I split off from the others and followed the humans back here," said Dahl.

"Is everyone else safe?"

"As far as I'm aware, they all got away up the river. They'll be halfway to Staunch Veil by now." Dahl paused. "Plumm was among them."

"Good."

The sound of hammering coming from the human camp interrupted them.

"Oh no," Tick hissed.

The humans were packing the carvings into a wooden shell – made from pieces of straight wood. They closed the shell and sealed the slabs inside with more banging and hammering. When the slabs were secure, one of the humans marked the side of the shell with strange symbols. Then they tied the jackals up close by to guard it.

Dahl's shoulders slumped. "They plan to steal the slabs away."

"What do we do now?"

Tick and Dahl stayed until all of the humans squeezed themselves into the last cocoon standing. They stayed until the human fire had died down to nothing, and still neither of them had worked out a plan.

Early the next morning, the film crew huddled round the fire, discussing plans. Ella stirred the hot chocolate. She'd slept terribly, all of them squashed together in the single remaining tent, with someone snorting and snuffling like a warthog. Ella suspected it was Walker.

"They said the chopper would be here before noon. It was lucky you had the satphone on you yesterday and didn't leave it here, Jack," said Ana.

"Then that's settled. Ella and I will fly back home with the slabs."

Ella stopped stirring. "We're going back?"

"Right now, those slab things are the best proof we've got." Jack poured himself a mug of hot chocolate and sipped it. "I want them under lock and key."

"I have to agree," said Ana. "We should get those artefacts back and then regroup. The likelihood of finding any further evidence in this location is virtually zero.

Those creatures won't be returning."

"Then the trip's over? But we just got here."

Jack saw the look on Ella's face. "I feel the same way. I wish we could stay and keep searching. But once we're back home, and have deciphered the writing on the slabs, I'll go to the studio and get them to fund another expedition. No shoestring budget this time. We'll return with a massive crew."

"I think they'll go for it," agreed Ana.

Ella tried to picture what their peaceful little clearing would look like swarming with people, more dogs and drones.

"Those yeti won't have a chance to escape a second time," said Uncle Jack as if reading her mind.

"But what if showing them to the world means putting them in danger?" said Ella. "What if they end up like the dodo or the moa, Uncle Jack?"

"Won't happen," said Jack.

"But what if it did?"

Jack smiled at her. "It's highly unlikely. Don't worry so much."

Ella took her hot chocolate and went over to sit near Shaan. Ella had seen the yeti first. She'd discovered them and she felt responsible. Now other people would come – many others – and she wouldn't even be there to see how it panned out. The yeti's fate was out of her hands.

"I don't really want to leave, Shaan," Ella whispered to the yak. "Not the yeti, not the mountain, not you."

But he just looked down at her with a blank expression and carried on eating.

★

"I've got it," murmured Tick. The two yeti were downwind of the human camp, flat on their stomachs, staffs by their sides.

"Please tell me you're thinking of something even remotely sensible," Dahl muttered.

"I'll let the humans see me," said Tick. "On purpose."

Dahl let out a groan. "As I feared…"

Tick carried on, undeterred. "The humans get a good look of me, and then they chase me. When that happens, I can lead them deep into the trees. Then you break into that shell somehow and drag the slabs away."

"Only one yeti has ever allowed herself to be seen on purpose, and we know how that turned out."

"Well, I can't get even more banished, can I?" said Tick. "Give me a chance to put things right. Please, Dahl."

Dahl chewed it over for a moment. "OK," he said at last.

"Really?"

"I can think of nothing better. But don't wave your arms or anything silly like that. If the humans believe you're trying to get their attention, they'll be suspicious. They must think they're in control. Humans like that."

"Got it," said Tick.

Dahl cracked his knuckles. "Are you ready?"

"What? Right now?"

"We've spent enough time waiting."

Tick took a deep breath and clutched his staff. To be seen on purpose! He needed a moment or two to prepare himself.

"Let's go," ordered Dahl. He got to his feet and picked up the Rumble Stick, Tick scrambling up after him.

Then a fearsome thumping came through the air, like the beating of a ghoulish drum. The yeti ran into the trees as a giant firebird swooped down the mountainside.

The last pair of humans had gone, following their yak and jackals out of the forest, before Dahl and Tick felt sure that it was safe to cross the river. It appeared the humans had abandoned their search for the sett.

The yeti inspected the clearing. "Not a trace. The slabs are definitely gone," Tick sighed.

"In the wooden shell with the firebird, flying south." Dahl slumped down on a log. He poked at the ground with the Rumble Stick, barely a hint of light in his eyes.

"What do we do now?"

Dahl shrugged. "I do not know."

"Maybe we could follow," suggested Tick. "The firebird looked like it flew towards the warmer lands."

"Did you see how fast it travelled? Even if we were able to find it, we would be many moons behind. And who knows where the slabs are heading?"

"Will they be able to read what's written?"

Dahl shrugged. "Not at first. No doubt our writing is as strange to them as theirs is to us, but they'll find a way."

"And then everyone will be in danger," said Tick. "Every yeti secret, every yeti law, the whereabouts of every yeti sett." He dropped down beside Dahl and began to sniffle.

Then a voice called out from the trees, "Hold your tears!"

Dahl and Tick yelped, tumbling off the log. There was a crackle of leaves, and a little yeti face pushed through the undergrowth.

"Plumm? Sweet fungus! What are you doing here?" Tick rushed over to her.

"After the humans chased us by the river, I followed you," she said to Dahl. "I thought you might need some help."

"That was foolish," grunted Dahl. "But also courageous."

"Well, I found a hiding place and watched the humans from the trees. To be honest, I got a little scared. I mean humans – right there! I didn't dare try to cross the river to find you. But sitting in my hiding place I made this." She handed Dahl a flat piece of tree bark with marks etched into it.

"What is it?" Dahl asked.

"The human writings. I copied them down as best I could."

"From where?" asked Tick.

"From the side of the wooden shell that the firebird took away. Wasn't that big bird scary!"

"I still don't understand," said Tick.

"I do, you clever yeti!" Dahl poked the tree bark with a thick finger. "This must be where they're taking the slabs."

"I'd say so," said Plumm. "You know how in the sett we write names on all the doors and tunnels telling us where things are? This is the same."

Tick peered at the strange writing. "Really?"

Dahl tapped the bark against his head as he tried to think. "We need to find a way of reading it… A yeti somewhere who speaks human."

"It still doesn't change the fact that we'll never catch up with the firebird, even if we tree-stride like the Earth Mother herself," said Tick.

Dahl clapped his hands together. "I have the answer. But it lies back at the sett. Come – quickly! Plumm, make sure you keep that piece of tree bark safe."

"It's good to see you, Plumm," said Tick as they strode back to the mountain, and raced towards the north face. "You were ever so brave to come back to help Dahl."

"I didn't really come to help Dahl, silly." Plumm wrinkled her nose at him. "I came back to help you."

When the three yeti neared the north entrance to the sett, Dahl growled to himself.

"What's wrong?" Tick asked.

"The entrance boulder. I hadn't thought of that. We'll never shift it – not with you two anyway," said Dahl. "No offence."

"None taken," said Plumm.

"The spreading tunnels," Tick blurted. "It's how I got out last night. When I saw the firebird."

"The spreading tunnels? But that's a restricted area. Is there anything you do that doesn't break the rules?" grumbled Dahl.

Tick led them downhill, into the forest, following his nose. He found the thicket he'd climbed out of before and rolled the much smaller boulder aside. The three yeti stuck their heads into the shaft. "It gets pretty tight in there, especially for those of us with large backsides," he said. "No offence, Dahl," he added.

Dahl snorted.

Tick pushed in first, on his hands and knees, and disappeared into the gloom, crawling uphill towards the fungusatory. He could hear Plumm shuffling behind him, followed by Dahl, grunting and complaining. At last, they reached the opening of the giant cavern.

Tick brought his palms together in a loud clap. The sound echoed through the chamber and, one by one, the glow-worms woke up. The little creatures turned on, and a wave of dim light crept over the walls and ceiling.

"What now, Dahl?" asked Plumm as soon as Dahl had squeezed himself out.

"First, we need supplies," he said.

Plumm and Tick followed as he headed off down a tunnel towards the larder, clapping the glow-worms awake as they ran. Nosh's pantry lay behind a thick curtain of moss.

"Let's hope Nosh left a few crumbs behind," Dahl said. He pulled a bag down and gave it to Tick.

"Dried centipedes," said Tick. He found a sack on the floor to put it in.

"Spider egg sacs," said Plumm, handing Tick a jar. "Ginger root, a couple of pine cones and some pine-needle biscuits – it's not much."

Tick climbed up to the top shelf and found a sack of onions hidden right at the back. "At least we have pudding."

Dahl shrugged. "It will have to do. Now let's go back to the farm. There's something I want to show you."

The three yeti padded downwards. It felt eerie moving through the empty sett. The air became heavy and damp, the tunnels narrowed and soon they were deep in the heart of the mountain.

In the fungusatory, Tick and Plumm followed the Guardian along the maze of paths that ran between the soft earth of the fungus beds towards the stream. There should have been a line of water carriers drifting towards the waterwheel, hanging up empty buckets, collecting full ones, but the rocky edges of the water channel were deserted.

Dahl stepped down into the passage carved into the rock and trod downstream – the water no higher than his shins. The others followed. Ahead, the channel carved its way through a tiny opening in the cave, and disappeared again into the darkness under a wall of stacked rocks. It was a dead end.

Dahl turned to the others. "Close your sacks and hold on tight," he instructed. "Make sure that tree bark is safe. Oh, and hold your breath too. The first bit's a little tricky."

Before Tick could ask why, Dahl took a step forward and disappeared under the water, air bubbles frothing above his head.

Tick stared down. "Wow!"

"Me next!" giggled Plumm, pushing ahead. Taking a deep breath, she pinched her nose and disappeared into the water.

Then it was Tick's turn. He clutched his sack and staff to his chest and stepped off the shelf, plunging into the cold water. At once, the current took hold, grasping and pulling with unseen fingers, dragging Tick deeper underwater. He bounced off the smooth tunnel walls, faster and faster. And, just when he thought he couldn't hold his breath any longer, the tunnel burst open into another cave.

In the weak light of the few glow-worms hanging from the cave roof, Tick could see Dahl and Plumm standing on the edge of the pool, waving him over. Tick swam towards them and stretched out a hand.

The dripping yeti stood in a large grotto, with a cluster of stalactites hanging from the ceiling. On one side, there was a thin shelf of flat ground. At the far end, Tick could see that the pool broke into streams heading off into the darkness. And sitting on the bank was a boat.

Tick had never seen a boat before, but he'd read about them in the *Encyclopedia Yetannica* at the library and seen a drawing. This boat was wide, with a flat bottom and low sides, and several struts running across it. He could see it was made of a single tree trunk, hollowed out in the middle by fire – a canoe was what they called it. The book said that yeti once migrated great distances in canoes such as these, paddling along secret waterways.

"It's been a long time," whispered Dahl almost to himself. He crouched down and inspected the sides, rapping his knuckles against the wood. He lifted out some paddles and examined them. "You two, scoop the water from the bottom."

"You've seen this boat before?" Tick said, shovelling water over the side.

"A long time ago. When I was just a fledgling. My

family came to the sett in this very boat."

"You weren't born in the sett?" asked Plumm.

Dahl shook his head. "My family journeyed from the lands of the south along these waterways. From the Mande Barung."

"The Mande Barung!" Tick's voice echoed through the cavern.

"My father was Mountain Yeti, but my mother came from the Mande Barung. Is there something wrong?" Dahl rumbled. He eyed the young yeti, eyebrows raised.

Tick shook his head. "No, no, of course not. It's just that I never knew. I haven't met a yeti from another sett before. I didn't know it happened."

"Well, it does." Dahl pushed the canoe into the stream and gestured for Plumm to get on board – holding its sides while she climbed in. "Well, it did once upon a time," he corrected himself.

Plumm grasped hold of the strut in front of her, not daring to move. Dahl gestured at Tick to get in the boat. It wobbled as Tick climbed in, threatening to tip over.

"Has anyone from our sett gone the other way?" asked Tick, setting down his sack and his staff.

"There was only one in my lifetime, many moons ago," said Dahl. He looked Tick in the eye.

"Mum," said Tick.

Dahl grunted. "When she was banished, Jiffi was of a mind to seek out another sett. I told her about the forgotten waterways."

"Where did she go?"

Dahl shrugged.

"Is she still alive?"

"I believe so, yes."

"How do you know?"

"I don't for sure," Dahl admitted. "But your mother was one of the best striders I ever saw, Tick. She's as clever as she is strong. If anyone could survive on her own, it's her."

Tick felt a rush of pride. He tried to picture his mother striding through the trees. But where exactly?

"This stream goes all the way to the Mande Barung?" asked Plumm, breaking the silence.

"Yes. There is one among them who can read human tongue," Dahl said. "A yeti as old as the trees. She will be able to decipher the writing on the bark. I'm also hoping that their sett still keeps messengers – we can trust them to spread the word. Now steady the boat while I climb aboard."

Tick and Plumm reached over to the rocky shelf and took hold as the big yeti clambered in between them. With Dahl on board, Tick felt the boat sink low into the stream.

"Take up your paddles. We must all paddle as one, and the current will help guide us. Plumm, we will follow your stroke."

Dahl untied the rope that held the boat against the shelf and, with a push of his hands, they drifted away from the rocks. Dahl dipped his paddle into the water and steered them into the dark hollow. He slapped the water's surface with the flat side of his paddle – like a clap – and the glow-worms came alive.

Ahead, the tunnel meandered through the mountainside, bending and curving, the ceiling high enough to be able to sit upright, the sides just wide enough for the boat to fit. Dahl gave the word, and Plumm dipped her paddle in the water, first on one side of the boat, then the other. Tick copied her movements.

"What's down the tunnel the other way, Dahl?" asked Plumm as she paddled.

"The sett of the Barmanou."

"So, let me get this straight," said Tick. "Each waterway connects us with a different yeti sett?"

"Stop paddling for a moment," Dahl instructed, "and look at the tunnel wall." He slapped the water with his paddle – much harder than before – and the glow-worms became brighter.

Tick and Plumm followed Dahl's outstretched finger.

On the cave wall, carved into the stone, was a symbol. It was a circle – like the Earth – that reached from the water's edge right up to the roof. And in the middle of the circle was a footprint. A large sole and four enormous toes.

"The International Yeti Collective. A union of nineteen mighty setts, each linked by waterways deep in the Earth. Once there was much travel between us, a sharing of knowledge. We were united."

"The Collective," murmured Tick.

They floated past, and the sign vanished once more into shadow. "What happened to the Collective? How come we don't hear about it any more?" asked Plumm.

"It's a sad history," said Dahl, laying his paddle across his lap for a moment. "Things began to unravel long before I was born. Each sett became so wrapped up in their own interests they lost sight of the greater good. Some yeti mistakenly thought it was better to go it alone. Soon setts stopped attending Collective meetings, thinking them a waste of time, until bit by bit, cycle by cycle, they were abandoned altogether. Cracks formed between us where before there were none."

Dahl paused and looked around the tunnel. "The Collective had more or less broken up by the time my family came to the mountain down this waterway. We were one of the last families to move between setts, and me just a fledgling, or so I was told."

Seeing his great hulk squashed into the boat, Tick couldn't imagine Dahl was ever a fledgling.

"I've often wondered what we yeti could achieve if the Collective were reborn," Dahl sighed. "I know in my heart that we're stronger together than apart. Particularly at times like this when danger lands at our feet."

"Then perhaps some good will come of visiting another sett," Tick said.

Dahl began paddling again. "Let's pick up the stroke. We have a long way to go."

Uncle Jack's place on the outskirts of Moss Gully was huge. More mansion than house, with a swimming pool and tennis court, surrounded by sweeping grounds that led up to the hills behind. In the basement, Jack had his own sound studio and editing suite. Ella was there to watch the crate with the slabs safely delivered by a team of removal people. Uncle Jack had used all his star power and more to get the slabs back from the mountains, the crate unopened. Ella was impressed.

Uncle Jack placed the carvings in the care of Dr Milligan, a linguistics professor. According to Ana, Dr Milligan was the best there was at ancient languages. All the same, Uncle Jack made the doctor sign a strict confidentiality agreement. No one was to hear a peep about the slabs until Jack decided the time was right.

Dr Milligan was so excited when he first saw the stone carvings, he had to have a little sit-down, a glass of water and a biscuit. Then, under his watchful eye, the slabs were each placed on tables in the studio and lit by soft light, like artefacts in a museum.

Now, finding herself in the basement on her own, Ella ran her hands over the stone. Her hands were touching where yeti hands had touched, she was sure of it.

"No touching!" hissed Dr Milligan, coming down the stairs. "What are you doing down here? These are not toys."

Ella blushed. "I know they're not. They're amazing."

The look of irritation dropped from Dr Milligan's face and the professor breathed in, eyes closed. "You can smell the centuries, the passing of time."

"Any idea what it's all about yet?"

Dr Milligan shook his head. "Deciphering an ancient language is not something you do in an afternoon, but I believe the language is not dissimilar to early Demotic."

"Demotic?"

"The ancient language of the Upper Nile – two and a half thousand years old." Dr Milligan pulled a magnifying glass from his pocket and peered at the slab in front of him. "See the individual chisel marks, each so precise? The writing – so delicate, so detailed? These are quite simply the archaeological breakthrough of the century."

"But we were up in the mountains. These aren't from the Nile – they're yeti."

"These carvings are the work of an ancient and

enlightened race of humans. Your yeti theory is too hard to swallow."

"We saw them," insisted Ella. "They definitely weren't human."

"But where's the evidence?" asked Dr Milligan. When Ella said nothing, Dr Milligan wagged a finger at her. "Interesting, isn't it, that for all the talk of yeti throughout history, we still have no proof? These carvings are probably Demotic, which is utterly remarkable in itself. Here, look at this."

He pointed out a picture. It looked like a map of the world – one of those olden-day ones where things weren't quite the right shape or in the right places. Ella fancied she could see the continent of Africa and across the world there was a blob she guessed was Australia. Next to the blob was a tiny speck. Was that New Zealand?

"This is the work of a sophisticated race capable of travelling great distances – possibly by ship. A nation of explorers, not hairy apes, I'm afraid."

"But Dr Milligan – I saw them. We all did," insisted Ella.

"An elusive Himalayan bear perhaps, a trick of the mind caused by high altitude," Dr Milligan snorted. "And, when my algorithm cracks the code, we'll find out which humans carved these slabs. Just a few more weeks, then your Uncle Jack and I will make a huge announcement."

Ella closed her eyes and saw the forest again, the mist, the yeti's sad expression, the fright written on its face. She remembered the jolt across her chest – it wasn't a feeling she would ever forget. She knew that if Dr Milligan managed to decipher the language, it would prove that she was right and that the slabs did belong to the yeti. But what then? The yeti deserved peace.

Ella wished she could warn them somehow. Give them a chance to hide. After her part in all this, it would be the right thing to do, wouldn't it?

Dahl, Plumm and Tick travelled down the underground stream. They'd been paddling for ages now along the channels with nothing but glow-worms and fireflies for company, and the occasional cave shrimp, which Tick found were crunchy and surprisingly sweet. At the back of the canoe, Tick acted as the rudder, dipping his paddle from side to side, steering the little boat clear of the rock walls.

"Take us over to that bank. Time to stretch our legs." Dahl's voice echoed along the tunnel, breaking the quiet.

Tick grunted, and steered the dugout towards the shelf of rock. The side of the canoe bumped against the stone and Tick took hold of it while Plumm looped their rope round a stalagmite. The canoe rocked, and lifted up in the water as the Guardian stepped ashore.

Dahl clapped his hands, waking up the sleeping glow-worms. A universe of stars suddenly dotted the ceiling. Tick clambered out of the canoe and then went to offer his hand to Plumm.

Tick peered into the gloom, looking for the ancient symbol painted on the wall of the cavern. There it was, on the other side of the water: a large sole and four enormous toes, the big foot. The ancient waterways may have become forgotten and disused, but it was good to know they followed in the footsteps of others.

"It's definitely getting hotter, isn't it?" Plumm said as she bent down and touched her toes. "I mean, when we started off, it was quite chilly down here, wasn't it?"

"We travel ever closer to the Mande Barung," said Dahl.

"How much longer?" asked Tick.

Dahl found a sturdy stalactite at the far end of the bank, and began to rub his back up and down along the rough stone. "A moon, maybe less."

"I can't wait to meet a Mande Barung! Are they like us?" asked Plumm.

"They look a little different, and do some things differently, but we are all kin."

"Spider eggs, anyone?" asked Tick. He rummaged in their sack of supplies and passed round an earthenware jar. The three yeti munched in silence.

Then the hair along Tick's back bristled. What he had

believed to be an extremely large and enthusiastic pair of glow-worms gave a blink. Now he spotted a second pair of glowing eyes, and then a third. All peering out from a corner of the roof at the far end of the cavern.

"I think someone's watching us," said Tick. He reached for his staff. At once, there was a flutter, a beating of wings, a high-pitched squeak, and the eyes were gone. "Bats." Tick shuddered.

"Sentries, gone to warn their friends that strangers approach," said Dahl.

"The Mande Barung?" asked Plumm.

Dahl pointed at the boat. "Back on board. We're closer than we think."

Tick crawled to his place at the back of the canoe. "I'm not a fan of bats. Gabb told me she had one caught in her hair once when she was out foraging."

"And you believed her?" laughed Plumm.

"Apparently, it was horrible."

"Enough, foolish yeti," said Dahl.

Plumm untied the rope and, with a push, they drifted into the middle of the channel, following the mysterious sentries and the flight of their leathery wings.

It took the best part of a moon after they met the bats to reach the Mande Barung. Paddle stroke after paddle stroke, taking it in turns to rest. At last, they reached another landing shelf, marked with the sign of the Collective. There they secured their boat and climbed upwards through the darkness, knees creaking. Dahl led the way, following his nose in the murk. The passageway had collapsed in places.

"Guess this tunnel hasn't been used in a while," said Tick as the three of them scrabbled at another mound of damp earth blocking their path, Plumm dragging the sack with the piece of tree bark behind her.

"We are the first in many moons," Dahl agreed.

The yeti managed to clear a small gap, and crawled through on their bellies. Tick stopped to eat a couple of earthworms he found wriggling in front of his nose. He passed one to Plumm.

Plumm slurped it down. "Hmm, spicy."

Back on their feet, they followed the meandering tunnel as it wound its way up to the surface. Then the passageway ahead began to brighten from deep black to grey as sunlight filtered down towards them.

"As of now, we're on the hush. Super-super-secret mode," Dahl whispered, poking Tick in the ribs.

"No snapping of leaves, no cracking of knuckles, no passing of wind, no nothing."

Dahl nodded. "We blend in with the trees like we're trees ourselves."

Ahead, they could hear the rustle of a forest and smell the air, unusual and pungent. And then came sunlight, reaching through a thick tangle of leaves. The yeti stopped and shielded their eyes. Dahl took a breath and parted the curtain of greenery. Then he stepped through.

The land of the Mande Barung was hot and sticky and, for three yeti from the mountains, a little too warm for comfort. It didn't take long for Tick to work out that their thick, woolly, mountain coats were not suited to the choking air of this place. Still, the three of them flowed through the trees, at one with the jungle. Whoops and whistles and screeches filled the thick covering above their heads. Cicadas buzzed and clacked as they sang their song.

They climbed up a steep ridge and followed its spine. Looking down over the sweep of the jungle, they could see a river not too far below them – this wasn't the raging snowmelt they were accustomed to, but a slow, sluggish waterway.

"What's that, Dahl?" Tick asked, pointing with his staff at the sweep of trees below them. One of them, right by the river – many lengths taller than the others – shook violently. It was as if someone had grasped the mighty tree by the trunk and rattled it from side to side. There was a pause, when the tree stood still, before it began again. The tree was waving at them.

Dahl dropped down the side of the ridge, heading for the tree, but when they reached the spot by the riverbank there was no sign of anyone at all. Dahl inspected the giant tree – giving it a good sniff – and seemed satisfied. "Mande Barung were here," he announced. "They watch."

"Well, they can watch me have a swim," Plumm chuckled. "I'm going in!"

"Not if I get there first," said Tick.

Dahl nodded his approval so Tick and Plumm dropped their sacks and clambered down the muddy bank through the thick reeds to the river's edge. With a sigh, they plunged into the brown water and rolled over on to their backs.

"You should come in! It feels so good to be cool," Plumm called out.

Dahl placed both hands on the smooth, rounded end of the Rumble Stick and rested his chin on it. "One of us must keep guard."

"He never relaxes," whispered Plumm, scooping up some water and splashing her face.

Tick shrugged. "He's the Guardian of the Sett. What do you expect?" After a while, he stood up in the water, feeling the squelchy mud between his toes. "That's enough – don't want to lose all my scent," he said, climbing out and sitting back down beside Dahl.

"Leech, anyone? I've got loads," said Plumm as she got

out, peeling a dark slug off her leg and popping it in her mouth.

"So where are the Mande Barung then?" said Tick after they'd been sitting on the bank for a while munching.

"They'll make themselves known soon enough," said Dahl.

As he spoke, there was a sudden rustling from the reeds along the riverbank and a loud slurping from the mud. Two towering shapes burst from the water, oozing filth. Tick reached for his staff as the beasts staggered up the slope, shaking muck from their fur.

Dahl got to his feet. "I was wondering how long you were going to wait down there, dear Twangg!"

"There's no fooling you, is there, Dahl?" said the mountain of slop. Twangg *(she who strums instruments)* ran a hand across her face and shook off the mud. "I thought we were well hidden."

"You were. I may have been a fledgling when I left, but I'd recognize your scent on that tree anywhere," said Dahl. He touched his hand to his chest, and then to his head. *"Take hold of the stone together and it will not feel heavy."*

"The first pancake is always a mess," replied Twangg, returning the salute.

She introduced the other Mande Barung. "This is Plott."

"Every vegetable has its season," declared Plott *(he who schemes)*. "We've been sent to fetch you."

"The bats from the tunnels told you of our arrival?"

"A moon ago. We've been watching ever since," said Twangg.

"These are my companions, Plumm and Tick," said Dahl. The two yeti also touched their hands to their chests and then to their heads. "We must meet with your elders. We come on a mission that is most urgent."

"Then let's waste no more time," Twangg said, leading the way back into the jungle.

"How did you manage to stay hidden underwater for so long?" asked Plumm.

"Hollowed-out reeds – you use them like straws," explained Plott.

★

The yeti followed the Mande Barung through the jungle. Twangg and Plott shook more mud from their fur as they strode between the trees. Tick reckoned they were about the same size as a Mountain Yeti, with long limbs and big padded feet, but their fur was shorter – more suited to the heat, he supposed. Their heads, however, were quite different. The Mande Barung were cone-headed. Just like a furry pine cone. That explained why Dahl's head was a bit cone-shaped too.

"Welcome to our sett!" said Twangg, coming to a stop at last.

Tick and Plumm looked around. All they could see were more trees.

"Look up," said Dahl.

They followed their Guardian's gaze. Up in the tallest branches of the tree above them was a giant nest woven out of branches and leaves, as if constructed for a large bird. And then Tick spied another, and another, until he could count more than a dozen. A cluster of leafy homes connected together by vines. In the centre was a large nest, twice as big as all the others.

"Our sett is always on the move," explained Plott. "We never rest in one spot for more than a moon or two."

Cone-head after cone-head emerged until a hundred eyes or more stared down at them. There were mothers with fledglings clinging to their fur, younglings with mischief in their eyes, and fathers who couldn't quite keep the look of suspicion from their faces. Tick and Plumm gave an embarrassed wave. Then from the largest nest came a shout of greeting, from a silverback standing tall.

"Do you bring *he who smells the fiercest*?"

"We do," said Twangg.

"I am he," declared Dahl, stepping forward and thumping the ground with his staff. "Dahl, holder of the Rumble Stick. Guardian of the Sett in the mountains to the north. *A big chair on its own does not make a leader.*"

"*Even a tiny star shines in the dark*," replied the silverback, returning the greeting. "Welcome, Dahl and friends. I am Cadd. As this is our home, so it is yours. Please join me and the elders in my abode."

A ladder woven from vines dropped down from the nest belonging to Cadd *(he who is sometimes a rogue)*. Plott held the ladder taut and invited them to climb. Dahl went first, then Tick and Plumm followed. Tick tried not to look down as he pulled himself up, staff between his teeth. The ladder seemed to stretch into the sky. When he finally pulled himself over the edge of the nest, he saw a group of elders reclining on mossy cushions on the nest floor, hands resting on large bellies.

The tree house was much more comfortable than Tick expected. Its curved edges rose up from the centre into a perfect backrest, covered with the softest moss. After the heavy stillness of the forest floor, it was delightfully breezy in the treetops, surrounded by leaves swishing like fans. There were clutches of berries, mangoes and nuts spread out, hanging just within reach. Tick suddenly felt very hungry.

Cadd caught Tick's stare. "Please, help yourself," he insisted with a kind smile.

Tick bowed his head and took a handful of nuts.

Plumm bit into a mango, crunching the stone between her teeth. "I could get used to this."

Cadd settled himself back. "I still remember the moon when your family left these parts, Dahl – though I was just a fledgling myself. It's a pleasure to welcome you back."

"I'd forgotten what a joy it is to lie in a nest of the Mande Barung," said Dahl.

"But I believe this is not a social visit."

Dahl shook his head. "I fear not."

The Mande Barung listened intently as Dahl told them of the troubles from start to finish. Tick's face burned like coals when Dahl recounted the bits he played a part in, but he noticed Dahl didn't mention him by name.

"I see," said Cadd when Dahl had finished. "This really does spell trouble. Never in my life has such a thing happened."

"Nor mine."

"But how can we Mande Barung help you on your quest?" asked one of the elders.

"Just ask and it shall be done," said another.

Dahl motioned at Plumm. "Youngling Plumm here was clever enough to write down what we think is the destination of the slabs. She copied down the human words from the shell they placed them in."

Plumm rummaged around in her sack, and found the precious piece of tree bark. Cradling it in her hands, she passed it over. Cadd studied the bark and gave it a good sniff.

"Our sett is ignorant of such learning," continued Dahl. "We need to speak with Leeke. Is she still among you?"

"The keeper of the slabs still tree-strides with the best of us," said Cadd, "though, with every passing cycle, she becomes…"

"More eccentric?" finished one of the other elders.

"Eccentric, yes," said Cadd. "But come, let us speak with her."

Tick had never seen a yeti quite like Leeke *(she who smells pleasingly like onions)*. Her hair was completely white, the cone of her head enormous and her eyes a startling shade of blue. Even though Leeke examined each of them as they gathered in her nest, to Tick it seemed like she was staring right through them.

"He who smells the fiercest, I'm glad to see you once more," Leeke chortled.

"And I you, she who sees all," Dahl replied.

"What is it you wish of me, malodorous one?"

"Please tell us, what does this say?" asked Dahl, handing her the bark.

Leeke studied the bark, her lips moving silently. "It is in human tongue," she pronounced at last.

"And?" prompted Dahl.

"Fragile. Moss Gully, New Zealand."

"*Fragilemossgullynewzealand?*" said Plumm.

"Fragile means likely to be broken," explained Leeke. "Moss Gully is the place. New Zealand is a name for the land – one of the human names for the home of the Makimaki."

"Makimaki?" asked Tick.

"Yes. Perhaps the most distant of Earth Mother's setts," explained Leeke. "Let us consult the carvings."

She rummaged around in the leaves behind her and pulled out a large bundle wrapped in soft bark. She undid the wrappings and put them to one side. Now, there in the middle of her nest, lay ancient slabs made of wood. Leeke inspected each slab in turn, before turning them over and studying the next.

Tick was puzzled. "Your slabs aren't carved out of stone like ours."

"Wood is lighter to carry when we move around," explained Cadd. "And easier to carve – if from time to time we want to make changes."

"You can do that?" asked Plumm.

"Rivers alter their course; seeds grow into tall trees. Things change. Why not our laws?" said Leeke. "The old ways teach us many things, but in life we should look into our hearts and then choose our own trail."

Tick was stunned. He hadn't heard an elder say anything like that before. He gave Plumm a look, one shaggy eyebrow raised. He could see his friend was just as surprised.

Then Leeke found the slab she was looking for. "Ah, here we are. The Makimaki. *And journeying along the south passage to the far reaches of the world travelled the younglings known as the Makimaki. To them were assigned the birds who stroll upon the ground, whose feathers are like silk, who shall never know the safety of flight…*

"Their land is known in human tongue as Aotearoa: land of the long white cloud. It is also called New Zealand," Leeke explained, tapping Plumm's piece of tree bark.

"Is the south passage the same underground waterway that brought us here?" asked Dahl.

"The very same," agreed Cadd.

"But didn't we already reach the end?" said Tick.

At this, Cadd and Leeke both chortled.

"No, no. The web of waterways is as long and as wide as the world itself." Leeke pointed to a map etched into the slabs showing a snaking line of tunnels. "First, you will need to pass through the land of the Orang Pendek."

Tick followed Leeke's finger as she sketched the path.

"To get to the Makimaki will take some paddling." Cadd whistled. "Never in my lifetime has one of our kind ventured that far."

"But it can be done," insisted Leeke. "*It is better to light a lantern than to grumble in the dark.*"

Dahl grunted in agreement. "Now, Cadd, I'm hoping your sett still has its messengers?"

"Yes, our treetop friends travel with us still." Cadd pointed to a nearby tree and Tick saw there were a dozen or so bats hanging there, their faces hidden behind dark wings.

"Then we need their help to ask the Makimaki to keep an eye out for the slabs, and to let them know of our arrival. We must also get word of our mission to Staunch Veil," said Dahl.

"Consider it done," said Cadd.

"There is another more crucial matter." Dahl paused, looking round the nest at the others. "We must alert all the other setts too. I believe the time has come to revive the Collective."

At this, Cadd sat up. "The Collective?"

Dahl nodded. "If we fail in our task and the humans decipher the slabs, then we can be sure that they will quickly learn the whereabouts of every sett on Earth."

Cadd let out a gasp. "Sweet fungus! I hadn't thought of that."

Tick shrank back from the sudden look of horror etched all over Cadd's face – a panic that would soon spread across the world. Tick felt sick to his stomach. He sensed a hand on his, and looked over to see Plumm giving him a quiet, comforting smile. Tick's eyes welled up.

"Every one of us might need to abandon sett," muttered Cadd as he came to terms with it all.

Dahl hung his head. "Just so. We must sound the alarm. And soon."

"Yes, wake the Collective!" Leeke cackled. "Wake the Collective! And not before time, if I may say so."

"Wake the Collective," Plumm repeated, trying the words on for size.

Cadd thought for a moment, then nodded. "Our bat companions will fly to every sett on Earth as if their own lives depended on it." He leaned over the edge of the nest and called out. "Friends, we need you. Please come at once."

One by one, the bats stirred, then dropped from their trees and flew over – giant wings beating – until the branches surrounding Leeke's nest were full.

Tick listened as, with one eye on the slab map, Cadd spoke to each bat in turn. As they received their instructions, the bats let go of their branches and flapped off through the trees.

"The word is spread," said Cadd at last.

Dahl bowed. "Thank you, dear friend."

"And now let us put aside our worries," said Cadd. "Tonight we honour your visit with a feast! After all, it is not every moon we get visitors from abroad."

Leeke licked her lips. "Will there be pickled geckos?"

That night, the Mande Barung gathered in the clearing in a big circle, with the Mountain Yeti as their guests of honour, flanked by Cadd and the elders. Tick hadn't seen any cooking fires or smelled any smoke coming from the jungle, but the larder keepers had prepared a huge feast, wandering in from the forest, bearing basket after basket of food. There were baked roots and boiled quail eggs. Pickled earwigs in jelly and barbecued crickets in mango sauce. Soon Tick's banana-leaf plate was heavy. Happy warbling rose up from the circle into the evening sky.

"Eat up, yeti, eat up. This might be your last proper meal for a time," chortled Cadd through a mouthful of fish.

Throughout dinner, Tick couldn't help but notice that Leeke's piercing eyes rested on him. Then, as the meal ended and the Mande Barung formed a circle to dance,

Leeke raised a gnarled hand and beckoned.

Tick pushed his leaf plate to one side and went over, kneeling before the wise yeti. Leeke popped a few barbecued crickets in her mouth. Then she ran a palm along his cheek, staring at Tick as if she was searching for something.

"You want to speak to me, O Leeke?" said Tick.

Leeke turned her attention once more to her plate. "It is not just the slabs you seek, is it?" she declared through a mouthful of pickled gecko.

Tick's heart thumped. "What do you mean?"

Leeke prodded him in the stomach. "This journey is about your mother as much as it's about the slabs."

"You know about that?" Tick gulped.

Leeke wiped her lips with the back of her hand. "She misses you too."

"How can you know?"

"I sensed it the moment you stepped into my nest – this feeling of great sorrow. I have chanced upon it before – you bear her scent."

"Where, when?"

"A yeti passed through this forest many cycles ago. Not far from the riverbank. A moon's striding from here."

Tick swallowed. "And you saw her?"

Leeke shook her head. "But only because she didn't want to be seen. I was out foraging when I felt a yeti pass by. I carried on picking herbs and waited for her to show herself, yet she did not. But her smell was the same as yours. Mountain Yeti mixed with sadness and shame."

Tick allowed himself a smile. "Then she's alive."

"There is no reason to doubt she still strides."

Tick sat in silence for a time, thinking of his mother, of her banishment, of her contact with humans. It reminded him of something that had been bothering him. "How come you can read human, Leeke?"

Leeke stopped eating for a moment and considered her answer. "Being able to speak other tongues draws beings closer, yes? It builds understanding."

"So, we should try to understand humans?"

"They were once our cousins – you must remember that," said Leeke. "Though many elders would think me a radical for saying so."

Tick reached over and took her hand. "Thank you, Leeke."

★

The following morning, on the forest floor a short stride away from the sett, the Mande Barung said farewell. One of the larder keepers handed Plumm a huge sack of provisions.

Plumm peered in. "More mango crickets – my favourite, yum!"

"And, to further help you on your quest, we have arranged a companion to join your party," said Cadd. He called to the treetops and down swooped a tiny bat on to his outstretched arm. "This is Flittermouse. You never know when you may need to send out a call, and she can guide you in the dark. She is our most trusted partner."

Of the three yeti, Flittermouse chose Tick to carry her, flapping over and landing on his shoulder.

Tick flinched at the feeling of her claws digging into his fur. He froze, his body stiff. Then Flittermouse nuzzled into his fur with her shiny nose, wrapping her wings round her like a tidy shawl. Tick looked down and saw that she was soft and dark, with large black eyes, and the fur on her face was flecked with brown. Perhaps he was wrong about bats. He gave Flittermouse a tickle under her chin and the bat gave a contented squeak. Tick grinned.

"Well, *a shrimp that sleeps gets carried by the tide*," declared Leeke, getting to her feet.

"Take care, Dahl," said Twangg, giving the Guardian a hug.

With steady striding, the yeti soon found themselves back at their boat, deep in the caverns below. The extra provisions made the boat sit low in the water. Dahl grunted with unease but Tick wasn't really thinking about the boat any more – he was staring down the tunnel. After what Leeke told him, he wondered if his mother had passed this way.

★

Ella had a yeti theory. It went like this.

The carvings they found in the mountains were something important – why else were the yeti trying to carry them away? On the carving that Dr Milligan showed her was a world map. What if the map showed all the yeti places – their homes? That would mean there were yeti all over the world. She needed to have another look.

Ella waited until Dr Milligan left for the day and then went down to the studio. She ran her hands over the carving.

South America. North America. Asia. Australia. Each continent had tiny squiggles of writing chiselled on to it. Her fingers found the tiny blob that looked like New Zealand. She touched the symbols. Were there yeti here too? Ella pulled out her phone and took a quick picture of the map. Then she went back upstairs, typing into a search bar while she walked: 'Yeti sighting NZ'.

There was an encyclopedia entry on cryptozoology, which Ella learned was the study of legendary creatures. There were also several websites about yeti. Then a link to an old article caught her attention.

Mysterious Hairy Creature
Reported on Greyton Peninsula
Greyton Daily, Tuesday, 9th February 1967

Explorer and would-be yeti hunter, Mr Ray Stevens, believes he has sighted another hairy, yeti-like creature, this time living in the bush country of the local ranges.

Out tramping near his home, Mr Stevens claims he saw a brief glimpse of a hairy man striding through the bush at great speed. While the creature left no tracks, there was, Stevens claimed, a noxious odour left behind, like that of rotten vegetables.

On investigation, Mr Stevens also maintains he found shells and bones in the ranges, proof he says of an unknown beast dwelling at ground level. Mr Stevens says that his findings tie in with local tales of strange night intruders in logging camps, and farm dogs growling at an unseen presence.

When asked to comment, Dr Bob Norris of Auckland Zoo said that it was highly unlikely that a primate or ape could inhabit the New Zealand ecosystem. Furthermore, members of the ape family were herbivores that mainly lived in nests in trees, and not on the ground. He found Mr Stevens' theory utterly implausible.

Dr Norris also pointed out that Mr Stevens' earlier attempts to prove the existence of yeti in the Himalayas were widely discredited. "I fear Mr Stevens is once again leading us up the garden path," said Dr Norris. "He's letting his imagination run wild."

Stevens – wasn't that the man Uncle Jack told her about? The one who took a photo of the yeti all those years ago and was later called a fraud?

Ella scanned the article again. "*Hairy man striding through the bush ... strange night intruders ... farm dogs growling ... unseen presence.*"

Uncle Jack's mansion was in Greyton Peninsula! That meant Stevens' yeti sighting took place in the hills right near here! Ella closed her bedroom door, her head full of questions. What if Stevens really had seen a yeti close by?

Ella walked up and down, trying to think. Dr Milligan said the creators of the carvings were highly intelligent. From what she had learned from her time in the mountains, Ella thought so too. So, if that was the case, perhaps there was some way she could communicate with them – warn the yeti what was happening?

"Maybe I could even help them get the slabs back," Ella murmured under her breath. She looked around to make sure no one had heard, even though she knew she was on her own.

Ella decided she needed to try and find these local yeti, if they existed at all. She would go up into the hills outside town and look for herself. Then her phone rang, startling her.

"Hey, Dad," said Ella. "How's the trip going? Where are you anyway?"

"In Perth this week. Just woke up." They chatted for a bit. "Listen, Ella. I'm afraid our trip is going to take a bit longer. The client is being kind of a pain," admitted Dad. "But we've spoken to Jack and he says you can stay on with him. Is that OK?"

"Sure, Dad, that's fine. I'm having a good time here."

"Glad to hear it. We'll make it up to you when we get back. Mum and I need this deal to go through, but after that we'll have more time to do stuff together."

"Sounds like a plan."

"Miss you."

"Miss you too, Dad," said Ella, but, to be honest, her mind was elsewhere.

The flock of bats flew out from the home of the Mande Barung in every direction. Some were as small as mice; others cast large shadows on the ground. They beat their wings, not stopping or resting until they reached their destinations.

The first bat swooped in as Sipp *(she who slurps when drinking)*, silverback of the Almas, fed a clutch of snow leopard cubs in their rocky den. The bat's teeth chattered as it squeaked its message.

"Trouble?" exclaimed Sipp as she wrapped her hairy red arms round the poor creature. She listened some more. "The Collective? On alert!" Sipp got to her feet. "Planke, Aspp, Gagg!" she shouted out. *(He who is thick; she with venomous tongue; he with many jokes.)* "The Collective wakes!"

★

"Take cover!" barked Inke *(he with stained fingers)* of the Sasquatch. The yeti from the squad of Rapid Reaction Volunteers ducked into the bushes as a pair of massive black wings flapped above their head. The bat landed on a tree branch and hung itself upside down.

"What do you see, Spratt?" barked Inke.

"Bat," Spratt *(he who eats no fat)* called out from behind a bush. "Greater fruit bat. Threat minimal."

The volunteers stood up. Inke came closer. "Strange to see such a bat this far north, eh, Grubb?"

"Very strange, sir," said Grubb *(she covered in dirt)*.

"What do you make of it, Spratt?"

"I think he's a messenger sent from hotter lands. Mande Barung sett, I'd wager."

"Mande Barung?" Inke rubbed his chin. "Now that's a name I've not heard spoken in years. Message, eh? What can it be about? Grubb, secure the boundary."

"Sir!"

"Ranke, some fruit, if you please. Quick, quick."

"Coming, sir." Ranke *(she who is rotten)* rummaged around in her carry sack and produced an apple, ripping it in two with her hands. She gave a piece to Inke.

The large Sasquatch held the apple up to the bat, who began to nibble. "First, you must finish your nosebag, my leathery friend, and then let's hear this urgent communiqué."

"Good grief! The slabs of the Mountain Yeti stolen!" muttered Inke a little later when the bat finished its peeping. "It looks like we're all in hot water. Back to the sett on the double," he ordered.

Cadd's messenger also swooped down on the mountains in a land to the north, seeking out a shadowy crevice, the secret entrance to the sett of the Greybeards. On hearing the bat's warning, Shipshape the silverback *(she in perfect order)* put the sett on high alert. All visits to the surface were cancelled until further notice. All peak-running was put on hold.

"If the humans learn of our exact whereabouts, we might even have to abandon the sett," said Shipshape.

"And what of our water purification?" asked Rainstorm, the Guardian *(he of damp humour)*. "The valley depends on us."

"I shudder to think," said Shipshape.

"Humans," grumbled Rainstorm. "Always trouble."

Crisp and Shrubb stared at the sand, the Yowies' fur camouflaged by the coarse tufts of grass covering the dune. The beach in front of them trembled, just a little at first, then the ripples spread outwards until the whole

147

area seemed to bubble and roll. A tiny dark shape coated in sand wriggled to the surface, then another. The turtle hatchlings forced themselves out on to the beach and, guided by an unseen hand, they crawled down the sand towards the sea.

"I just knew it was hatching time," said Crisp *(he baked in the sun)*.

"Swim, little ones, swim," said Shrubb *(she smaller than a tree)*, keeping an eye on the sky for hungry seagulls. "Look out!" she cried, spotting a large dark shape. She leaped out to protect the turtles as a large bat swooped down into the clearing and landed on a nearby tree.

Shrubb let out a relieved sigh as the bat began squeaking at them.

"Mountain Yeti?" Crisp took a deep breath, listening to every word. "On a quest? The Collective?"

"As soon as all those hatchlings are in the water, we'd better stride," said Shrubb.

At the far end of the Earth, a yeti of the Makimaki sett opened his cupped hands, revealing a tiny brown bird with oversized feet and a nervous disposition.

"Go on now. Time to make it out there on your own," whispered Songg *(he with tuneful voice)*.

The young bird tottered on the soft, spongy earth, and

eyed the shadows with suspicion. It tested the dirt with its pointy beak – like a needle. Then all at once came a thrashing of large wings from above and the bird fled, vanishing into the undergrowth.

Songg stared up at the giant messenger, puzzled. "Bat? There are no bats that size around here."

He listened to what the bat had to say and then called out to the silverback nearby. The bat beat her wings and disappeared once again into the night.

Dunkk *(she who dips biscuits)* slipped through the bushes. "What was that? I heard something swoop through the trees."

"A messenger. And you're not going to believe what she had to say. We're about to have visitors."

Greatrex sat at the head of the Council table in the great hall of Staunch Veil and listened to the messenger, his blanket drawn round his shoulders, his staff tapping out a steady rhythm on the smooth stone beneath his feet.

The silverback felt his heart lift as he listened to the bat's squeaks. Though the troubles of the yeti were far from over, now at least there was some cheer.

"So, Dahl and the younglings are safe and follow the slabs?" asked the silverback. "And the Collective is revived too – well, well."

The bat squeaked in confirmation.

"Now that is welcome news," said Greatrex with a small smile. "But you must be hungry after flying all this way."

The bat squeaked that this was so.

Greatrex beckoned to the yeti standing guard at the entrance to the hall. "Please take our little friend to the larder and see she gets a proper meal, and then somewhere warm to sleep. She has brought us such important news."

The three yeti swept along in the canoe, the current drawing them further and further towards … who knew what? Plumm and Dahl slept, their heads resting on either side of the canoe, which left Tick alone with his thoughts, and the gentle breathing of Flittermouse, who snuggled into his fur.

Leeke had known about his mum.

She could have travelled down this very tunnel, couldn't she? said the idea fly. *Could be this water is bringing you two closer and closer.*

I sense it too, replied Tick.

The boat drifted in the darkness for a short time before they came to another stopping place, the sign of the Collective chiselled into the cave wall. Near the sign, Tick saw an opening that led to the surface. He tied the boat up and breathed in. His nose twitched. He was sure he could smell ashes and fire.

Take a look. It could be something important, said the idea fly.

I seem to remember you've said that before, Tick complained. But something wasn't quite right, he could feel it.

Tick glanced at the sleeping yeti. Should he wake them? They looked so peaceful. Besides, he didn't fancy Dahl getting up on the wrong side of the canoe.

He climbed out of the boat, grabbing his staff. Before leaving, he made sure the boat was secure, then padded up the tunnel, the smell of cinders getting stronger with each step. At last, he reached the tunnel entrance, the opening blocked by a boulder. The stone wasn't too big, and he shoved it to the side, bit by bit. Tick stuck his nose into the gap and inhaled. On the wind came the pungent reek of embers and broken earth.

"I don't like this, Flittermouse," admitted Tick. Hanging from his hairy back, the bat peeped in agreement.

As soon as Tick squeezed through the gateway, the smell of burnt wood struck him. He pushed the boulder back into place. Tick could see a path working its way through an outcrop of rocks. He held his breath and threaded his way through. Then he broke out on to the hillside.

Fire.

Flames engulfed the hill, devouring the forest, roaring,

spitting, snarling. Branches snapped, embers shot through the air – a firestorm of red and orange. Fire raged through the tallest of the trees, their limbs shaking and moaning. Beyond the flames, just visible through the wall of heat, lay a ruined landscape of tree trunks, shattered and lifeless. More burnt trees than anyone could count, flung down like an army of corpses – the ground below scalded black, scorched and choking in ash.

Tick considered the animals that called this forest home. Soon they would have nothing left. What of the local yeti? Tick saw that if he could clear a barrier through untouched forest before the flames got there then he could save some of the hill. But he and Flittermouse were all on their own. Rushing into things had landed him in trouble before.

Tick hesitated for a moment, then he charged, swinging his staff like a club, beating bushes down as he went. Tick lunged at the shrub nearest him, grabbing hold of the branches. He pulled with all his strength, ripping roots from the ground. Sparks singed his fur, the heat relentless. Flittermouse squeaked in terror. Tick grabbed another bush and heaved, but there were too many to rip out. He had come too late.

Tick spun round to go back and met a barrier of fire. It had swept in behind them, blazing across the hillside surrounding the boulders further up the mountain. All around, there was nothing but flame.

"Flittermouse! Find a way!" Tick yelled.

Tick watched as the bat disappeared into the smoke, pursued by flying embers. He backed away from the flames, the island of untouched hillside he stood on getting smaller and smaller.

Flittermouse swooped back down, wings beating above Tick's head, buffeted by the current of hot air. She gave off urgent squeaks.

"Straight down the hill? Are you sure?"

Listen to the bat! screamed the idea fly.

Tick stared in horror at the blaze in front of him. Were they really asking him to plunge into that?

Tick backed up as far as he could, away from the raging fire surrounding him. Flittermouse hovered above his head, squeaking. She meant for him to follow her, but the yeti stared in terror down the hillside at the flames towering into the sky. A few trees remained, somehow still standing dark and strong as the fire raged round them.

Tick held his staff out in front of him and took off down the hill, following the bat's path. Then, before he could stop, he was at the wall of flame – he could hear screaming in his ears before he realized it came from his own throat. Tick picked out first one dark tree trunk, then a second, like islands in the fire. His fur crackled, his eyes stung, but the trees called him on, guarding him from the full force of the inferno. If ever there was a time Tick was glad to be a tree-strider, it was now. Down the hill he sprinted, his feet barely touching the burnt soil, his staff swinging at the flames, beating them back. Acrid air reached down his throat, squeezing his lungs. And with a last scream, just when he thought he could bear it no longer, he was through. Tick stumbled out into the blackened land left behind by the fire, and rolled around on the smoking soil, thrashing at his singed fur. He lay there, gasping for breath, but he was safe. Flittermouse clicked and whistled above his head, and swooped down – landing on his shoulder.

"I owe you," panted Tick. He struggled to his feet. Looking back, he tried to pick out the secret path between the boulders, the way back down to the waterway. He couldn't even see the rocks for flames. The last few remaining trees of his escape route were burning now. Tick would have to wait for the fire to run its course, and then try to get back down to the waterway. Dahl and Plumm would wait for him, he hoped.

Flittermouse gave an urgent squeak. "What do you mean humans?" said Tick. He turned and peered at the valley through the smoke. Then he saw it. A cluster of dwellings, the sound of thumping, a gathering of huge yellow beasts with circles for legs and ... humans. Tick crouched down low, close to the ground. He watched as a gang of humans followed the flames' path on foot, clomping through the stubble of burnt bushes. They wore dark coverings over their eyes and wrappings over their mouths. There was a horrible whining, and then a charred tree trunk toppled to the ground, cut down. Tick gulped. Did the humans destroy this forest? But why?

One of the yellow beasts ploughed up the hill towards him, circle legs turning fast, bellowing and wailing as it climbed. Tick saw humans inside, urging it on. Had they seen him? There was nothing for it but to run.

Tick kept low and ran further down the hill, away from the waterway, away from Plumm and Dahl, towards the untouched jungle in the distance, Flittermouse flapping above. This time he was glad for the smoke that wrapped itself round his body, keeping him out of sight. He fled for the treeline.

Down in the basement at Uncle Jack's house, Ella watched as Ana and Walker began filming once again. They'd only been back in the country for a few days, but Uncle Jack was impatient to get going.

Jack leaned over one of the slabs and gazed at the camera. "Ever since I trekked back from the Himalayas with this treasure, I've worked tirelessly to learn the secrets of the yeti. It's lonely work, down here on my own with nothing but these carvings and my thoughts. But I guess it's part and parcel of being on a yeti quest." Jack paused, his voice getting more hushed. "Today I think I may have cracked it. I'm starting to believe these slabs are in a language not dissimilar to Demotic, the ancient script of the Upper Nile. The web of mystery gets thicker and thicker."

"Cut!" said Ana. "That's a wrap. That'll do for this scene. Walker, get some close-ups of the writing, and then let's do some exterior shots."

"We're getting close, I can feel it," Jack said. "Milligan has almost worked out the slabs. The yeti won't be in the shadows much longer."

Ella could see she was running out of time. To carry out her plan, she needed to get up into the hills and find the yeti without drawing attention to herself, and she reckoned she knew just how.

Later that day, she asked Uncle Jack to drop her off at the train station at the bottom of the hills just outside Moss Gully. The miniature train with its little engine and bright green carriages was a favourite for tourists – taking people up the winding track into the hills and bringing them back down. Ella told Jack she'd always wanted to go.

"Now are you sure you don't mind if I don't come? It's just that I'm still kind of busy today with the shooting schedule," Jack said.

"I'll be fine," insisted Ella.

Once she'd bought her ticket, Ella went out into the train yard, found an empty carriage and climbed in.

A couple of tourists joined her and the driver closed the metal gates on each carriage with a clang. Then, with a lurch and a screech of wheels, the train pulled out, the engine at the front puffing. Straight away, it began to climb the hillside, the bush close enough to touch. On both sides of the small train, Ella noticed saplings, hundreds and hundreds of them. The train driver explained over the speaker that the railway owner and his team planted them as a way of bringing the hills back to life.

The train climbed higher and higher, passing into the hills through one brick-lined tunnel after another, Ella snapping photos along the way. At last, they reached a tall wooden viewing tower.

The bush spread out beneath them, dense and green, with tree ferns fanning their fronds like umbrellas. In the distance was the coast and beyond that, through the haze, Ella could make out islands lurking in the sea. She waited until all the tourists had clattered up the stairs before crossing the train tracks and heading away into the bush. The last train left the viewing station at four. That gave her two hours. Not much time.

As far as she could work out from the cryptozoology pages she'd studied online, there were many possible signs of yeti. Stacks of rocks, trees shaking, broken branches, nests on the ground like those for giant birds, hollows or caves, horses with their manes plaited. It didn't seem like anyone could agree on what yeti got up to.

Ella pushed on through the bush, a sweet almost peppery smell to the air. She passed by giant trees with trunks like ships' masts, their bark dappled with silver. Dark vines criss-crossed the bush like hair. Ella made a note of her bearings – working out how to find her way back to the train – and carried on, finding her own path through the trees.

It was dark in the bush now, though beams of sunlight streamed through gaps in the canopy. Ella was glad to be in the cool. Soon she heard water tumbling and found herself at a stream trickling over rocks and boulders, tumbling into a pool. Ella sat by the water's edge and scanned the hillside around her. *This is nuts*, she thought. People had searched for yeti hiding places for years with no luck. What could she do in just one afternoon?

She was about to give up and go back up the hill when something caught her nose. It wasn't the spicy smell she'd noticed before, but it was familiar. Ella closed her eyes. There was definitely a stink. A bit like a rabbit's hutch. A bit like the lost-property box at school when it was full of shoes. Now where had she smelled it before?

Ella opened her eyes. *The Himalayas!*

She tried her best to follow the smell but it wasn't easy. She'd never followed one before. At times, it seemed so close and at others it disappeared entirely. For once, she wished she had a bigger nose.

Ella kept to the edge of the stream, heading down the hillside. And then she spotted a cave entrance carved out by a channel of water, hidden behind thick fern fronds. Just above the surface of the trickling water was a pile of river rocks, neatly stacked, one on top of the other.

Ella gasped. "Rock stack!" She found a hiding spot in the bush where she could keep an eye on the hollow and settled down. She checked her watch – she had just over an hour to make that last train.

Barely making a sound, Ella sat and watched the opening to the cave. But there was no sign of anything. On closer inspection, Ella was beginning to have doubts about the stack of rocks. Perhaps they'd been dumped by the river? They could have been sitting there forever – all covered in moss like that. But then again that stench was no coincidence. She was sure it was a clue.

Ella glanced again at her watch. She needed to get the train back down the hill. She'd have to come back soon and try again. Before she left, she took a few photos so she'd recognize the place.

"Nice train ride?" asked Uncle Jack when he picked her up. "See anything interesting?"

"Oh yeah, the view from the top is amazing," said Ella. "I want to go again."

Hidden in the jungle, Tick and Flittermouse watched for hours as the yellow beasts with circle legs tore through the burnt remains of the forest, pounding and hammering the ground. Tick gaped in horror as the humans churned up the earth and tried to flatten what was left of the hillside. What of the tunnel and the waterway below? What about Dahl and Plumm – were they still safe? It had been ages since Tick had got out of the boat – would they have waited all that time? Tick knew he had to reach them. But he just wasn't sure how with the humans about.

Flittermouse! thought Tick. Why didn't he think of her before? She could take a message – tell Dahl and Plumm he was on his way.

"Hey, Flittermouse," Tick blurted, about to ask the bat to fly back up the hill. But then he remembered the boulder covering the entrance – that he'd so carefully put back in place. There was nothing for it but to get back up there himself.

Finally the humans headed back down to their sett. Tick still didn't move. He waited until darkness before leaving the forest. Then he bounded up the hillside, finding his way back through the charred skeletons of the trees, Flittermouse flapping at his shoulder. Tick squeezed himself in between the cluster of boulders at the crest of the hill and found the entrance to the waterway. Checking to see there was no one watching, he heaved the boulder aside. Tick climbed into the tunnel and pulled the boulder back in place.

As Tick squeezed himself through the tunnel down towards the waterway, he pictured Plumm and Dahl waiting for him, the boat bobbing on the water. How they'd greet him and Flittermouse, how he'd clamber back in the boat and carry on the journey. But, when Tick got there, the chamber was dark and empty.

Tick clapped his hands to wake up the glow-worms and in an instant he saw the cavern was ruined. Great piles of earth almost filled the hollow, brought down by the humans and their contraptions flattening the earth above, though water still managed to flow along the channel. One thing was sure: there was no boat, no Dahl and no Plumm.

Tick groaned. His friends must have stayed for as long as they felt they could, and then, with soil and rocks tumbling down on their heads, Dahl would have made the call to escape. It was the right call too, thought Tick. He couldn't have expected them to risk their lives and wait. Now he and Flittermouse were truly on their own.

Tick's first thought was to dive into the water and swim with the flow, chasing after the boat. With Flittermouse guiding the way, he might catch them. He stepped to the water's edge, gripping the rock with his toes, but something held him back. He crouched down to force himself to think. Dahl and Plumm were probably long gone – far away down the dark tunnel. He wasn't the greatest swimmer either. He would need a boat to have any chance of catching them. Tick wasn't sure he could build one – to start with, it would take time, and to build a boat he'd need trees, which meant several trips down into the untouched forest and back up again. Too risky.

Tick tried to remember the map from the slabs that he'd seen in Leeke's nest. He was fairly sure the Orang Pendek sett lay to the south. Could he try to get to them and ask for help? Call on the Collective? What had Dahl said? Stronger together.

"What do you think, Flittermouse? Think you can get us to the Orang Pendek?"

The bat gave a chirrup. She reckoned she could.

Tick scrambled back to the hillside and drifted through the darkness, down towards the forest. Once in the trees, he picked up the pace and strode south, his staff gripped in his hand. He kept his eyes on Flittermouse as she darted through the cover of green. "I hope you know where you're going, my friend."

Tick ignored the ache in his feet, the stiffness in his knees, and strode from tree to tree. It felt like a lifetime since he had left Plumm and Dahl asleep in the boat that morning and he was exhausted. "Just a little bit longer, Flittermouse," he panted.

But soon, when his striding became noisy and careless, and he could barely put one big foot in front of the other, Tick knew he had to rest. He came to a stop and leaned against a tree, looking for somewhere safe to sleep. He peered up the tall trunk. He could try to build a nest up high, like the Mande Barung. Flittermouse seemed to think it was a good idea, swooping to the top of the tree and latching on. Tick took a deep breath, and used the last of his strength to haul himself up. He began bending the green branches together, trying not to break them, weaving them into something resembling a nest. But, before he could finish, Tick lay down and fell asleep, Flittermouse on his shoulder.

★

Tick woke up with the chattering of the birds. Flames, blackened trees and beasts of yellow filled his mind. But then he realized that he was safe, high up in the treetops, Flittermouse clinging to his fur. Tick had a knot in his back where a branch had been digging in all night, and his neck was stiff. His feeble attempt at a nest would make a Mande Barung blush.

A strange smell invaded his nostrils. Tick sat up with a start. He wasn't alone. He spun round in his nest, and there on the branch next to him sat a yeti. A very small yeti.

"I was wondering when you were going to get up," said the yeti. He ran his hands through the shock of black hair that tumbled down to his waist. He found a nit and popped it in his mouth. "I'm Strut. *When warthogs fight, it is the grass that suffers.*"

"*A small cloud can hide the moon.*" Tick touched his hand to his chest and then to his head and introduced himself. "Orang Pendek?"

"That I am."

Tick beamed. "You don't know how happy that makes me. I've been looking for you."

"Well, now you've found me."

"You see, I'm in a bit of trouble. I need a boat. I need to

find my way back to the waterway."

"Do you know what Orang Pendek translates to in human tongue?" asked Strut *(he with bouncing walk)*. When Tick shook his head, Strut went on. "'*Short person*'! I mean, really! Why not 'strong arms' or 'magnificent hair'?" Strut lifted up his fringe and peered at Tick. "Tell me honestly now, do you think I'm short?" He got to his feet, balancing on the branch.

Tick looked the Orang Pendek up and down. Even standing, Strut's head was not much higher than Tick's and Tick was still sitting in the nest. He had never seen such a small yeti. "Of course not, no," he insisted.

"I mean they could call us 'protector of the forest' or 'defender of the tiger'. That would be closer to the truth. But short?" Strut snorted.

"Foolish humans," said Tick.

"You said it."

Tick paused. He didn't want to be rude but he was in a bit of a hurry. "Thing is, like I mentioned, I really need to get underground. To a waterway."

"Not sure if you've ever seen an orangutan. Now that's what I call short. And what do you think their name means in human?"

"I have no idea," sighed Tick.

"'Person of the forest'," snorted Strut. "'Person of the forest', a noble name like that, and they come up to here."

Strut patted his shoulder. "Titchy."

"You're probably right," said Tick. "Now, about that boat."

"I brought you some breakfast," said Strut. He handed Tick a gourd with thick, prickly skin. "You need to peel it."

Tick hadn't realized just how hungry he was. He dug his fingers in and ripped off the skin. At once, the treetop filled with the most pungent of smells – an overpowering stench of rotten cabbage, and onions, and goats. The smell wrapped itself round Tick, running through his fur like fingers with just the right amount of nail. Tick felt dizzy with pleasure. He pulled off a piece of flesh and began eating. Flittermouse flew off in disgust.

Strut pointed at the disappearing bat. "Your friend? I had one like that come and visit just the other moon. From the Mande Barung. Told me the Mountain Yeti are in a serious kerfuffle. On some sort of quest."

Tick put down his fruit. "That's me – that's me! I'm Mountain Yeti."

"Well, you should have said."

"Funny that," said Tick, getting to his feet.

Strut started to plait a strand of his hair. "So what's the plan?"

"I need to find the waterway and a boat," Tick

explained. "I'm going south."

"Yowie country?"

"No, Makimaki."

"Don't know a lot about them," said Strut.

"Me neither until a few moons ago," admitted Tick. "Can you help me?"

Strut finished his plaiting. "Oh yeah. No problem. The waterway is close. I'm sure there's a boat – I heard someone talking about one once."

"You don't know how happy it makes me to hear you say that."

"Give us a piece of that," said Strut, taking the fruit from Tick.

After breakfast, the two yeti clambered down the tree and Strut took the lead, using his strong arms to pull his way through the undergrowth at great speed, his long hair flowing behind him. Flittermouse threaded her way through the trees above. Tick followed as best he could, sticking to the little yeti's trail. Low-hanging vines whipped his head as he moved and his face was scratched by leaves.

It didn't take Strut long to come up with the goods. In the green of the jungle, on the path ahead, was a boulder, flat and grey. Strut took a quick look around and then scampered up the smooth rock on all fours, Tick following.

"There," said Strut. "The waterway."

Below the bridge of rock was a river, its water green and still. So still that not a single ripple creased its surface. It didn't make a sound. It barely looked to be moving as it drifted through the jungle, tree branches dipping into the water. The river was deep and dark, and to Tick's eyes the best thing he'd seen in moons.

"Strut, you beautiful, long-haired wonder!"

Strut beamed and ran his fingers through his hair.

Beside the river, Tick saw there were branches full of the spiky, smelly fruit, like hornets' nests hanging from thick stalks. There was a splash as one plunked into the water. It sank into the green, then bobbed up to the surface and floated away.

Tick wondered if he should gather a few of the fruits for his journey, but Strut had already scurried over the bridge and down the other side of the boulder, swinging himself underneath and using the ridges in the stone like a ladder. Tick scampered after him, and the two yeti lowered themselves down towards the water's edge. In the shadow of the overhang, Tick saw a crack in the rock, and beside it a neat pile of stones. They were here then.

Strut made sure there were no prying eyes and then wedged himself through the gap. Tick sucked his tummy in and followed.

The fissure was deep, dropping steadily downwards – soon it became too dark to see at all, and Tick made do by following the sound of Strut's feet and the peeps of Flittermouse. Then, at last, the gap opened up into a cavern. Strut clapped his hands together and the glowworms woke up. When Tick saw the big foot chiselled into the wall of the cave just above the flowing river, he grinned. He looked around the cave for the boat. A murky shape sat on the water, further down the cavern. Tick raced along the bank of the waterway. It was a canoe, full of water.

"You've done it again, Strut!" Tick slapped his companion on the back. Now Tick could see himself aboard his new boat, riding the current, paddling smoothly, Flittermouse guiding the way. He saw the moment his boat caught up to Dahl and Plumm, the astonishment on their faces.

Tick turned to Strut. "Give me a hand getting it out." He took hold of the bow, and directed the smaller yeti to the other end. Together, they lifted. There was a crack, and the yeti were left holding two pieces of rotten wood.

Strut stared down at the hull which was rapidly disappearing. "I don't think it was meant to do that. I guess it hasn't been used in a while." He took a handful of his long hair and twirled it into a topknot.

Tick sat down with a thump on the riverbank.

Flittermouse flapped down to his shoulder and hung from his fur, squeaking.

"What are you going to do now?" asked Strut.

Tick sighed and shook his head.

"You can always stay with us," said Strut. "Wait till you meet the others. We're all a bit spread out now the humans have cut down the forest, but my best mate Mould is a real laugh."

"I'm sure he is," said Tick.

Strut picked at Tick's hair. "We'll have to do something about your hair if you're going to stay. Will it grow longer than this?"

Get up, fly – get up! Tick shouted inside his head.

He could hear the fly beginning to buzz. *Boat sunk? Then we go back up to the jungle. We do it on foot.*

Too far, way too far. Also, we'd have to swim across a massive ocean.

Then we carve out a new boat.

Not enough time.

How about we tie some logs together?

We'd never get them down here through the crack in the rock.

The fly fell silent. *Then we do it on foot.*

You already said that one.

Strut broke the silence. "Now then, we might as well get something to eat. Plenty of fruit by the river."

Tick thought back to the hanging fruit – the *plunk* as

it dropped into the water. The fruit floating downstream.
"You're a mastermind, Strut!"

"Really?"

Tick got to his feet. "We need lots of spiky fruit, we need some vines, and we need them fast."

Strut smiled. "Mastermind. No one's ever called me that before."

20

Tick finished lashing another spiky fruit to the raft. He counted about twenty now. The raft was almost there – a few more fruit and he'd be ready to push off. It wouldn't keep him dry but it would float. Tick guessed Dahl and Plumm were halfway to the Makimaki already.

"Keep 'em coming, Strut!" Tick shouted down the tunnel. "And some more vines too, please!"

Soon Strut reappeared, his arms full of fruit, vines wrapped round his chest. He dropped the pile of fruit to the floor of the cave, then kneeled down and helped Tick arrange the large gourds in a row. He held them in place while Tick tied their stalks. Then, using the leftover vines, Tick bound the whole lot together.

"That should do it," he said. "Did you ever see such a fine raft, eh, Strut? Now let's launch her." Together, the yeti heaved the fruit raft over to the stream and dropped it in the current. Tick made sure he held on. The raft bobbed up and down, the dark water burbling underneath it.

"Look at that!" exclaimed Strut. "You'll be there in no time."

Tick grinned. "Let's hope so. You ready, Flittermouse?" The bat dropped down from a stalactite and landed on Tick's chest.

Strut whistled. "I've never met a Makimaki. Really ought to one moon, I suppose."

"I'll make sure to say hello from you," said Tick, tucking his staff under a vine.

"I wonder how tall they are…"

"Probably not very. And I bet their hair's really short."

"You reckon?" said Strut. He began plaiting another long strand of his own.

"Thanks for everything, Strut," said Tick, giving the yeti salute. "*With patience, even the ant can eat an elephant.*"

"*A good buttock deserves a comfortable seat.*"

Strut held the raft steady against the bank while Tick climbed aboard. The young yeti lay on his stomach, his legs dangling off the end. Tick pulled out his staff and felt for the bottom of the channel. By shoving against the bottom on each side, Tick reckoned he could steer.

"Off we go!" he cried.

Strut gave the raft a push, and Tick and Flittermouse

drifted into the darkness, carried onwards by the current. When they were out of sight, they heard the Orang Pendek's voice calling after them:

"...atch ... ut ... or ... th ... s ... ake!"

Flittermouse gave a puzzled squeak.

"Sn ... k...!" came the shout again.

Tick shrugged. "Probably something about hair."

He pushed himself into a fast rhythm, dipping his staff in one side and then the other, guiding the raft of spiky fruit down the channel. The raft was surprisingly stable, and, when his legs tired of kicking, Tick found that it would take his entire weight if he sat upright.

Not bad at all, thought Tick. He calculated that he was probably a moon behind the others, possibly two. The fire had cost him time, as had the finding of the waterway and the need to build a raft. But if he kept this pace up he might just catch them. As he propelled himself along, using his staff, Tick worried about whether the humans had worked out how to read the slabs yet.

★

In the studio in Jack's mansion, Ella got out of the way as Dr Milligan hurtled towards his computer on the far side of the room, the wheels on his desk chair squeaking along the floor. The doctor had called them all down for the big reveal. "Finally I've cracked it!"

There was a part of Ella that couldn't wait to find out the secrets behind the flowery writing, to know all there was to know about the magical yeti. But, once the mysteries were out there, there was no returning. This genie couldn't go back in the bottle. Jack would share the yeti secrets with his TV bosses. Then the studio would send a huge crew back up into the mountains, and, while the whole world watched, Uncle Jack would chase the yeti into the open.

Dr Milligan punched the keyboard urgently, then he sat back, polishing his glasses with his tie.

"Well?" demanded Jack. "We've been waiting days for this."

"Patience, Mr Stern, patience. We're on the verge of cracking one of the most important linguistic conundrums ever."

Ella focused on the little wheel in the centre of the computer screen, her head a muddle of anticipation and dread. Suddenly the wheel stopped and the screen went blank.

"What's it doing?" said Jack.

"This is it, ladies and gentlemen!" said Dr Milligan.

A text box flashed on to the screen:

`Learn one strange ancient way to younger skin.`

Dr Milligan jabbed again. Nothing. He waggled the mouse. Nothing.

`Learn one strange ancient way to younger skin.`

"You've got to be kidding me. Yeti skin products?" said Jack.

Dr Milligan wiggled and jabbed some more. "Shhh!"

`Learn one strange ancient way to younger skin.`

"Come on, Dr Milligan, let's get cracking!" demanded Jack.

"Shhh, please!" pleaded Dr Milligan, poking at the keyboard.

`Learn one strange ancient way to younger skin.`

"Looks like a virus," said Ana.

"No!" Dr Milligan banged the keyboard with his fists.

`Learn one strange ancient way to younger skin.`

"Aaaaaargh," moaned Dr Milligan, his eyes misting over. "All my work."

Ella let out a sigh of relief and then quickly checked to see that the others hadn't noticed.

Tick calculated a moon had passed since leaving Strut, without so much as a breath of fresh air or a glimpse of sunlight, only the glimmer of the ever-present glow-worms above his head. The raft squeezed itself through another tight gap, banging on one side of the tunnel and then the other.

Tick dropped his legs into the water and kicked, the

sound echoing down the tunnel. The raft picked up speed, hurtling along, knocking into the rocky walls and carrying on. Then up ahead, in the darkness, Tick saw a flicker of light on the surface of the water. A small flicker but enough to catch his attention. The glimmer reappeared for a moment and then disappeared. There was something in the waterway.

Tick hauled his legs out of the channel. The raft groaned, water sloshing over the top. He sat upright, as close to the centre as he could, holding on to the vines with one hand, his staff in the other, and they flowed over the spot where the flicker had been. There was nothing.

Tick breathed a sigh of relief – it was just his eyes playing tricks on him. "False alarm."

Then the raft shuddered, and suddenly pitched to one side. Flittermouse screeched as she escaped into the air. Tick plunged into the dark water and spun round, scrabbling for the raft, hands searching. His fingers closed round a vine. He heaved, kicking out at the water, clawing his way to safety along the spiky fruit. A glistening shape broke the surface to his right, carving through the water with a hiss, then it was gone.

Tick felt something wrap round his legs, thick like the trunk of a tree. It took hold and tried to wrench him from the raft. He held on with all his strength. Flittermouse swooped down and grabbed his fur, her wings beating, trying her best to help, but it was no use. Whatever held Tick was too strong.

Tick plunged under the surface, the creature wrapping its way round his body. He could feel slimy skin and powerful muscle. Tick still held on to his staff but he couldn't raise it. His arms were pinned. He screamed, air bursting out of his lungs. He saw the head of the beast now, the stony eyes, the wide jaw, the cold, expressionless face. Tick heard Strut's voice again. Too late, he understood what the yeti had been trying to tell him. *Watch out for the snake! Snake!* He felt too dizzy to fight any more. So this was how it ended.

Then the serpent let go. The coils unravelled in a flash and it shot off into the darkness. Tick burst to the surface, chest heaving. He spun round in the water, trying to get his bearings. The raft was gone, the snake too.

Tick dugs his toes into the rocky bottom of the channel. With his free hand, he felt for the tunnel wall. It was too slimy to hold on to and the water sucked at his legs, stronger than before, pulling him on.

Then a gargling sound reached out through the darkness, growing louder. It built up until it was a steady howl, bouncing off the tunnel walls, a roaring that seemed as if it was all around. Tick had a nasty feeling inside.

"Flittermouse – go and look!" he said. The bat soared off down the tunnel as Tick turned round and tried to swim in the opposite direction, his arms pulling, his legs kicking. It was no use.

Flittermouse returned, trilling urgently.

At the same time as he heard the word 'waterfall', Tick lost his fight against the current. He banged against the side of the tunnel, barrelling downstream. Then the young yeti seemed to hang in the air for a moment, before dropping, screaming, into the void.

Tick tried opening his eyes but his eyelids were like stones. There was a desperate throbbing in his head and his shoulders ached too. He struggled to lift his hand to his face and felt along the side of his head. His fingers found a large bump and pulled back as pain rushed down his neck.

Tick remembered the angry pull of the current. He remembered a scream and flying through the darkness, and not much after that. Where was he? Taking a deep breath, he propped himself up on his elbows. He could hear the rushing of water – his fur was still wet, the river close by. Tick's fingers reached across the damp stone and felt his staff by his side.

He rolled on to his back and clapped his hands, making his head ring. The glow-worms woke up. Using his staff to keep himself steady, Tick pushed himself up on to

trembling feet. In the gloom, he could see his raft – or
what was left of it – smashed against the rocks. Above the
wreckage, there was a big foot carved on to the wall. A
squeak came from Flittermouse, hanging from the cave
roof.

"Just about, I think," Tick replied. "You?"

Flittermouse peeped back. She was fine, and there was a
way out to the surface.

"Show me."

Flittermouse dropped from the hanging rock and flew
towards a deep crevice in the stone. Keeping one hand on
the rock wall, Tick edged his way uphill after the bat, each
step sending a jarring sting to his head.

Further on, Tick could see the gloom lightening a
little. Flittermouse flew onwards and Tick rested, panting
against the rock, waiting for her to come back. After a
short while, the small bat returned to report that the coast
was clear, and that it was night.

Tick inched through the narrow crack and out into the
open. He breathed in, glad of the fresh air. It was a jungle,
that much he could tell. The scent of damp soil, of rotting
leaves – the strange pungent reek of unseen flowers – it
all spoke of the land of the Orang Pendek. They hadn't
travelled that far at all then. Tick listened for sounds of
the humans' yellow beasts but there was nothing above the
chirrup of crickets.

What to do? He would rest somewhere safe, then see about another raft. He had to keep going.

Tick's eyes adjusted to the gloom and now he could make out dark shapes ahead in the jungle. He ducked behind a tree as quickly as he could manage, blocking out the agony in his head as he gawped at the strange figures. They still hadn't moved. He took another deep breath – there was no smell coming from them. Flittermouse peeped down from the canopy above.

"An empty dwelling? Are you sure?" Tick leaned on his staff and crept through the forest towards the strange shapes. If it was a dwelling, he'd find shelter there. When he was close enough to touch one of the dark shapes, he found they were made of stone. Tumbledown dwellings carved from rocks, most likely human shelters once upon a time. Tree trunks thrust their way through the walls, vines grasped at the stone, so that the dwellings were now more jungle than anything else. Tick pushed through a clutch of vines and stumbled into the darkness, seeking a hidden corner. He was too weak to search further. Tick found a dark corner, and lowered himself to the ground, grateful to rest his head.

Then, through half-closed eyelids, Tick caught sight of a large shape moving through the shadows – creeping towards him between the vines. He raised himself to face the shape ... and blacked out.

★

Tick woke up, wincing at the glow of sunlight, and immediately shut his eyes. Everything was fuzzy. He remembered stumbling out of the cave, finding the strange ruins in the jungle. Then he vaguely recalled that something had come towards him in the dark. With a start, Tick forced his eyes open again and sat up.

There it was! A figure by his side – a blur. A yeti smell. But the effort of sitting up was too much for him and he fell back down.

"Try and keep your eyes open, Tick," a voice came to him, as soft as lichen.

"Plumm?" said Tick. He blinked a few times but still couldn't see. "I caught up to you!"

"It's not Plumm," said the voice.

"What happened?" mumbled Tick at the blurry shape. "Where am I?"

"Among the ruins. I discovered you last night – your bat said the snake got you, and then you were swept over the waterfall."

Though he hadn't heard it in many, many moons, the voice sounded just like his mum's. That must have been one serious knock on the head.

"You sound like my mother," he whispered.

"That's right, Tick. I *am* your mother," said the voice.

Tick felt a hand stroke his cheek and warm lips on his forehead. A pungent smell invaded his nostrils; of pine sap and earth, of sunshine on rock, of mulberry jam and fungus. Tick sat bolt upright, the pain forgotten, and his eyes wide open.

"Mum?"

Leaning over him was a kind face with lively green eyes, a gentle brow ridge, a bottom lip that stuck out just a little – like that of a curious youngling – and a shock of red hair circling her head, soft and long.

Jiffi gazed at her son with tears in her eyes. "Yes, it's me, Tick."

"But how? I thought you were…" Tick threw his arms round her. "Oh, Mum. I've missed you."

"Not as much as I've missed you," murmured Jiffi, squeezing hard.

Mother and son held each other tight. The warm squash of her arms, the soft breath, a kiss, and Tick knew she was real. This was real!

"Where are we, Mum?" said Tick finally, wiping his eyes.

"The ruins of the human sett – my home, in the jungle, a few moons from where the Orang Pendek live," explained Jiffi. "I landed here many cycles ago, same as you, washed up by the waterfall. Your friends too."

"Dahl, Plumm? They're here?" Tick could hardly believe it.

"They're out foraging. They'll be back soon. We've all been very worried about you."

Tick lay back down. "Did they tell you what I did?"

"They told me about the slabs."

"I've made such a mess, Mum."

"I heard about what happened on the mountain. I've also heard how brave you've been to track down the carvings, how you put yourself in harm's way just to get them back. I've heard it all."

"I've been a foolish, stupid yeti, Mum."

"We all make mistakes in life, Tick. It's how you respond to them that counts," said Jiffi. She leaned down again and hugged him tight.

"I always knew I'd see you again," said Tick.

"Me too," said Jiffi.

The entrance to the cave darkened. "Lazing about while others work, why am I not surprised?" came Dahl's deep voice.

Tick stiffened.

"He's just joking," said Plumm, appearing beside him. "You big meanie," she added.

Tick heard Dahl chuckle. Then the huge head of the Guardian leaned over him, blocking out the light, Flittermouse perched on his shoulder. "It's good to see you again, foolish yeti," he said with a chortle. "Let's hope that rock knocked some sense into you."

"Good to see you too, Dahl."

Flittermouse chirruped and Tick lifted a hand to scratch under her chin. He found it hard to believe he hadn't liked bats once upon a time. But then he'd never met Flittermouse.

Plumm came over and squeezed his shoulder. "We were so worried when we woke up and found you gone the other moon," she said. "What happened?"

Tick sat up and Jiffi handed him a coconut shell filled with water. "It started with a fire," Tick explained, taking a long drink. He told them all about his adventures. From battling the forest fire, to the human contraptions, to Strut and the raft of spiky fruit.

"And the firestorm you saw, can you explain it?" asked Dahl.

"I'm not sure," said Tick. "But it seemed as though the humans were doing it on purpose."

Jiffi sighed. "Some humans burn the forest to clear space to grow their oil trees. It's been going on for some time."

"Oil trees?" asked Tick.

"Palms with nuts on them. They crush the nuts to make oil."

"How do you know so much?" asked Dahl.

"Lots of time on your hands when you're banished," said Jiffi. "I do what I can to rescue the animals, but against the fire and the yellow beasts with circle feet I have no defence."

"They were terrifying, I don't mind admitting," said Tick.

"Well, I hope you'll be well enough to travel in the morning," said Dahl. "The new boat is ready – we have time to make up."

"I'll be ready," Tick insisted.

"The good news is that Jiffi has travelled these waters before and can help point us in the right direction," said Dahl.

"You're coming with us?" Tick began to smile.

"Silly question," Jiffi replied. "I'm never letting you out of my sight again. Ever."

When Tick was feeling well enough to walk, Jiffi took
him to have a look round her home. In the sunlight,
Tick gaped at the ruins of the human sett. They seemed
to stretch on forever. Jiffi led him along the winding
paths that worked their way through the stone skeletons,
Flittermouse darting and weaving.

"Humans built it a long time ago and then abandoned it
to the trees. No one knows why. It belongs to the animals
now."

Jiffi stopped and showed Tick a stone wall. "But they
made some beautiful things – look." Chiselled into the
wall was a forest scene. A tree with branches full of tiny
teardrop leaves; a trio of storks strutting in a dance, long
necks stretching to the sky; a pair of monkeys eating
fruit while, on bended knee, a human cupped his hands
together and bowed his head in admiration for them all.

Jiffi traced the shape of the human with her fingers. "People aren't all tree burners, that much I know."

The way the human in the carving looked at the animals made Tick think of Pebble Nose. "What really happened with you and the humans?" he asked. "I need to know."

"I'll tell you about it later, I promise."

Tick found an animal with a long nose carved into the stone. "Is that an elephant?"

"Yes, there's still a few around."

Jiffi lifted Tick's hands from the stone and gazed at them. "You've got your father's hands. Big lumpy fingers."

Tick dropped his head. "If only I'd met him. Just once."

"You did meet him, Tick. He used to hold you in his arms every chance he got," said Jiffi.

"I wish I could remember."

Jiffi took his hand again. "Come, let me show you." Tick followed his mum towards the sound of water murmuring over rocks. Jiffi stopped at a shallow pool of clear water fed by a gentle stream. "This is the clearest, stillest pool in the jungle," she explained. "Kneel down on the bank and stare at the water."

Tick got down on his knees, and did as his mother asked. It took his eyes a few minutes to adjust, but in the surface of the dark pool he saw a young yeti staring back at him, a mother looking over his shoulder.

"You see those kind eyes?"

Tick gazed at the water and nodded.

"They're your father's eyes. The way your face crinkles up around them when you laugh – just like your dad. Your nostrils flare up just the way his did when he was excited. The big brave head – full of questions – exactly the same." Jiffi turned Tick round. "You may not remember meeting him, Tick. But he's there with you all the time."

"It's been really hard not having either of you around," said Tick.

"I wanted you to be safe," Jiffi said, her eyes filling up with tears.

"I guess we're here together now, aren't we? That's what matters," said Tick. He gave her a hug.

Jiffi wiped her damp face with the back of her hands. "Now how about something to eat, Flittermouse?" she said, smiling at the little bat who hung in the tree above them. "I know where you can get the best guava in the whole forest." Taking hold of Tick's hand, Jiffi led the way.

★

In the morning, Jiffi took the other three yeti down along the rocky stream bed, and towards a deep gorge where there was an entrance to the waterway big enough to get the boat through. Dahl and Jiffi carried the new canoe above their heads. Tick and Plumm brought the food sacks and paddles. Hanging over his shoulder, Dahl had what remained of Tick's spiky fruit tied together with vines.

The gang of yeti trudged ankle deep into the river and headed towards the darkness, Flittermouse flying ahead. Following the course of the stream soon brought them to the waterway itself and the walls of rock closed in around them once more. As they lowered the boat on to the water, Dahl seemed pleased to see that it floated. They pulled it along until the water was deep enough for the boat to drift fully loaded. Flittermouse hung upside down from the roof of the cave.

"I hope we don't come across another snake," Tick muttered.

"Don't worry, they won't cross the waterfall – they're too scared," said Jiffi.

Dahl kneeled down and tied the spiky fruit to both sides of the boat. "I'll take the front and Jiffi the back. Younglings in the middle."

"Do you know these waterways?" asked Jiffi. Dahl shook his head. "Then perhaps I should go at the front."

Tick saw Dahl stiffen. Then he relaxed. "Yes, that's a good idea."

"Jiffi, have you been to visit the Makimaki before?" asked Plumm.

"No, but I've been close," said Jiffi. "I hear they're a good bunch."

Dahl held the boat steady and gestured for Tick and Plumm to get on board. Then Jiffi quickly made herself comfortable at the front. Dahl spread the sacks out along the length of the boat. Finally the Guardian stepped gingerly into his place at the back. Even with the spiky fruit tied to the sides, the boat sat worryingly low in the river.

"Let's hope we encounter no more rapids," Dahl said as he untied the rope and pushed away from the bank. They began drifting with the current at once, Jiffi setting the stroke, Plumm and Tick following her paddle with their own.

"Hard right, Dahl," Jiffi commanded as they reached a fork in the tunnel.

"Right it is," said Dahl.

For a long time, the four paddles worked with the current, and the boat sliced through the water, the yeti not saying a word. Tick could tell they were making good time, not stopping to rest. They passed several Collective signs without pause, taking it in turns to doze in the boat when they felt tired. Above their heads and a thick layer of rock was an ocean, deep and wide. Once across it, they would be in the land of the Makimaki.

★

"I'm bored," announced Plumm, her voice breaking through the darkness.

Dahl groaned. "Not this again."

"I think we should have stopped and had a chat with the Yowie when we passed by," said Plumm. "It seemed a bit rude not saying hello."

"You spend your whole life never seeing another yeti sett, and now you worry about social calls?" said Dahl.

"Maybe on the way back," suggested Tick.

"Just saying," said Plumm.

Tick dipped his oar in and pulled. "How much further, Mum?"

"Not long, a couple of moons at the most."

"Why don't you tell us now?" said Tick.

"Tell you what?" asked Jiffi.

"About getting banished."

"You've heard it all before, haven't you?" Jiffi sighed. "Broke the slab laws – seen at a human dwelling, consorting with a human. Putting the sett at risk – almost bringing the whole world tumbling down on our shaggy heads?"

"That's what everyone says," admitted Tick.

"There are two sides to every story."

"Then what did happen?" asked Tick.

Jiffi fell silent and gave a few more paddle strokes.

"I was a moon's striding from our sett, low down in the mountains, gathering a different fungus spore for the fungusatory. I was foraging in the undergrowth when

I sensed something upwind. Something rustling in the bushes. And then I saw her."

Jiffi paused for a moment. "Dark hair, deep brown skin the colour of a nut – no more meat on her than a bird. A human child. Through the thin cloth covering her body, I could see just how frail she was, how fragile. That's what she was – a fledgling bird fallen out of its nest. The child was lost, and a long way from her sett in human strides. As the girl sat there, sobbing, wet streaks crept down through the dirt on her face, like rivers of sadness. When your father passed away, I shed them too – I'll never forget. I stared at her for a time, and the longer I watched, the more I knew I needed to do something to help her. There were jackals all around and night was close. It wouldn't take them long to find her. How she'd survived out there until then, I did not know. But I hardly dared to move – I mean, to approach her, a human! I would have to risk everything. If anyone found out, I'd lose my life in the sett, life with my son."

Tick felt a lump building in his throat.

"So, I made a hard choice. No yeti would turn their back on the smallest bird – why then a human? We were cousins once upon a time, weren't we? I knew I couldn't leave her. And, when I emerged out of the bushes, to my astonishment the girl wasn't frightened. Not in the least. She smiled at me. Do you know how humans smile? They show their teeth like this." Jiffi turned round and lifted her upper lip, baring her yellow teeth.

Tick and the others giggled at her contorted face.

"A human smile means they're happy and want to be friendly – same as ours," explained Jiffi. "Next thing I knew, the girl flung her arms round me and buried her face in my fur. Can you imagine? Here I was, several times larger – capable of tearing her limb from limb – and she had opened her arms to me. I could feel her heartbeat through my fur. I knew in that moment that humans are capable of great trust. In her heart, she was no different from me, from you. The elders don't tell us all that."

Tick thought back to the forest and the way Pebble Nose and he had made contact. He'd felt it too.

"So I slowly gathered my nerve," Jiffi continued. "I reached down and picked her up as if she was no more than a basket of fungus. As far as I knew, no yeti had ever embraced a human before. I felt the girl go limp in my arms with relief. She was happy.

"It didn't take me long at full stride to reach the human sett with its walls made of mud, and its cows. The child had fallen asleep in my arms some time before. Making sure the way was clear of humans, I laid her gently down outside the front door of a dwelling, banging on it with my hand, and I fled. I was gone before any other humans saw me."

"So then what happened?" asked Tick.

"I was discovered," Jiffi sighed. "To this moon, I can't explain it. Another yeti out foraging? Perhaps I'd been followed? Word soon reached the Council. The elders confronted me, and, though some things they had heard were false, I couldn't deny that I'd been with the humans at their sett. I tried to explain why but they ignored my words. The punishment was carved in stone."

"I should have shown more trust in you," Dahl sighed.

"You weren't to blame, Dahl. If it had been you at the human dwelling instead of me, I would probably have been just as shocked." Jiffi turned round and squeezed his hand.

"Then what?" asked Plumm.

"The worst decision you can imagine. To leave my son behind. I decided the safe arms of the sett were a better place for a fledgling than a life of banishment. I knew as well that Dahl would see that Tick was cared for."

"So that's why you're always on my case," said Tick. Dahl grunted.

"And you turned out well for it," said Jiffi.

"That's a matter of opinion," Dahl muttered.

Plumm laughed. Then all of a sudden they were all laughing, their chortles echoing down the tunnel.

"Well, I think you made the right choice," said Tick, his

laughter dropping away. "Both times. I don't care what the rules or the elders say."

Jiffi stopped paddling and wiped her eyes. "Well then, that's all that matters. Now perhaps we should send Flittermouse to fly on ahead. Let the Makimaki know we're coming?"

"Good idea," said Tick. He woke up the tiny bat and spoke to her. Flittermouse peeped that she understood. Then she flew off into the darkness, leaving the boat far behind.

The first sign of the Makimaki wasn't a Collective symbol, or a watching bat, but a song that floated through the darkness like dandelion fluff. It was the most tender and beautiful yodelling Tick had ever heard. The yeti lifted their paddles out of the water and just listened.

There is but one Earth, from which all things flow,
From glittering sea to freezing snow,
From mountain high to dark caves below,
Oh, there is but one Earth, from which all things flow.

A web carries all, like a net made of vine,
The shrimp, the ray, the shark combine.
Flower's nectar, bird beats her wings,
But pluck the bloom, does she still sing?

Sunshine, rain, wind, from which all things flow,
There is but one Earth, this much I know…

The ocean tides flow constant and faithful,
Waters of life – learn to be grateful.
Waste in the sea swirls like a cloak,
Wraps round the turtle, making her choke.

Sunshine, rain, wind, from which all things flow,
There is but one Earth, this much I know…

When the last tree in the forest is turned into wood,
And the fish that swim are gone for good,
When the rivers turn sour like dark sewer ditches,
Will humans at last learn that they can't eat riches?

Sunshine, rain, wind, from which all things flow,
There is but one Earth, this much I know…

"I think we've arrived!" said Jiffi.

The Makimaki chorus gathered in a large cave, their fur blending in with the dark stone walls that rose up high. Hollowed-out gourds kept up a gentle beat, long-necked instruments strung with hair thrummed and twanged, while the leader waved his long arms up and down like an ocean swell. At the sight of the boat approaching, he dropped his hands and the music stopped.

The Makimaki clustered round the edges of the cavern, all eyes on the approaching boat, the younglings curious and whispering. On first impression, the Makimaki weren't very different from Mountain Yeti, Tick noticed. Their fur had a bit more red in it, their arms were longer – hanging down right to their knees – and their fingers were longer too, like thick twigs off a tree. Dahl guided the boat to the landing, and two Makimaki rushed over and tied it up.

The yeti climbed out of the boat as the Makimaki elders came forward to greet them.

"Welcome, O cousins from the mountains. *If you kick a stone in anger, you hurt only your own foot*," declared the silverback, leaning on her staff. "I am Dunkk. Are you Dahl, he who smells the fiercest?"

"It is I," replied Dahl. "*The sun which melts wax also hardens the clay.*" He introduced himself and the others.

"Just as our sett is our home, so it is yours. Hear me as I speak." Dunkk touched her hand to her chest and then her head. Jiffi, Tick and Plumm returned the salute.

"The song of the Makimaki is indeed sweet," said Dahl, addressing the cavern. "It allowed us to forget for a moment the task that lies ahead."

"You are too kind, dear cousin," said Songg, the leader

of the choir. He gave a signal to the Makimaki chorus, and they filed down the tunnel towards the sett.

"We have heard of your quest from the messengers of the Mande Barung, and your bat was most helpful too," said Dunkk.

Now Flittermouse dropped down from above, swooping round the gathering. Tick stretched out his arm as a perch, and Flittermouse landed, chirping and squeaking.

"Hello, Flittermouse," Tick said, and tickled the bat underneath her chin.

"Now join us at our table – there is much to discuss." Dunkk took Jiffi and Dahl by the arm. "I'm afraid things do not look good."

The cavern was packed. At the head table sat Dunkk, Songg and the Council Elders alongside their guests. Tick noticed that every bench in the cavern was full, the Makimaki casting polite but curious looks at their guests while they munched on cicada pie with snail gravy.

With a twinge, Tick remembered the last time he had sat in such a full meeting hall, in their own sett. The time they drew the stalks. If only his stalk hadn't been chosen. If only he'd listened.

Dunkk pushed her plate to the side, ready to talk. She examined the piece of tree bark that Dahl had given her. "Well, you have come to the right place," said Dunkk.

"The human sett they call Moss Gully isn't far. Since word came by bat from Mande Barung, we've been keeping an eye on their dwellings, hoping for sight of your slabs. Sweet fungus, how we've hoped for something."

"My scouts and I have spent many moons on the edge of the forest," added Songg.

"And?" asked Dahl.

"Not a thing."

"In truth, we didn't have much to go on," admitted Dunkk. "But unfortunately we now have a new and bigger problem."

"Bigger?" asked Jiffi.

"We fear our own sett may have been discovered by humans."

"How?" Tick barely had the strength to ask.

Songg sighed. "We are not yet certain. It may be that the human youngling stumbled upon us by accident. We're not sure she truly knows we're here – that's the only reason you find us still in our sett and not in our retreat."

"Youngling?" asked Dahl.

"We think she rode the green beast with many circle legs, then found her way here through the trees. Our sentry observed her sitting in the bush and watching," said Songg.

Tick felt his heart thump. "A girl? What does she look like?"

Songg shrugged. "A human girl. A youngling. They all look the same but she has a very small nose."

Tick sat bolt upright. He shoved his plate and Plumm's to one side, clearing a space on the slab of rock.

"Excuse you!" said Plumm.

Tick waved her away. He bent down and felt around on the floor of the cave for a stone. Then, as the table watched, he began scribbling on the surface of the eating bench. Long hair, a slightly round face. Peering eyes. A pebble for a nose.

Tick finished his drawing. "There."

"Who's that?" asked Jiffi.

Dahl peered over. "It's the girl from the mountain."

Dunkk and Songg inspected Tick's picture. "Yes, that's her! The one who watches." Songg took a deep breath.

Tick sat back down. "Pebble Nose. Dahl is right. She was with the humans that tried to discover our sett."

"But how has she come here?" asked Dunkk.

"By firebird," answered Plumm. "She and the silverback climbed in with the slabs and flew away. We saw."

"And now this youngling is at our very door," grumbled Dunkk. "I do not like this."

"We must abandon sett," barked one of the elders, thumping the bench. "Give the order."

"Let's not be too hasty. She hasn't yet ventured into our cave, neither does she look dangerous," said Songg.

"All humans are dangerous," said another elder. "*A cobra will bite your rump whether you call it cobra, or Mr Cobra.*"

Dunkk shook her head. "That's not entirely true. What of the humans we see in these parts planting trees and caring for the forest?"

At this, the elder just grumbled.

Now Jiffi spoke up. "But you say this youngling comes alone, and hasn't returned with others?"

"Not so far."

"Then perhaps she doesn't want to bring ruin to the sett – if, as you say, she even knows it's here," Jiffi pointed out.

"True. At the mountain, they brought special jackals to seek us out," Dahl agreed.

"I wish I shared your optimism." Dunkk let out a long breath. "Her being at your mountain and now here in our bush is all too much of a coincidence for my liking."

"But don't you see? At least now we have a way of finding the slabs," said Plumm. "We just have to follow the girl and see where she goes."

"Plumm is right. If we keep a lookout for her, Pebble Nose is bound to lead us to the place where they keep the carvings," said Tick.

Dunkk grumbled. "I don't like it."

"It's our only chance of finding them again," Tick insisted. "Let's hope she pays you another visit."

Upwind and uphill, Tick, Songg and Flittermouse sat watching in silence, eyes locked on Pebble Nose. The yeti stared as she clomped through the bush and nosed round the cave before perching in the undergrowth to spy. She was as reckless as a wild boar, thought Tick, the way she crashed around, snapping twigs and snorting and snuffling.

It now seemed beyond doubt that she was here to find yeti, but this time her manner was different. Up in the mountains, the humans gave chase and wanted to hunt the yeti down. Here there was no thunderclap stick, and no jackals. Pebble Nose was doing her best not to intrude. Tick also remembered the way she had cared for the yak.

But it was not something he could communicate to Songg sitting beside him. They were on super-super-secret mode. Tick pointed at Pebble Nose and drew a slab in the air. Songg understood.

When Pebble Nose became tired of watching without reward and climbed back the way she'd come, Tick and Songg followed. They crept through the bush, arms down by their sides, hands swinging low, Flittermouse flapping high above. Songg led Tick towards the strange tracks of the green beast that wound their way back and forth down the mountainside. They stopped and waited for the creature with circle legs to come clattering along. As the beast chuntered into view below them, Tick had to admit that humans were capable of making some amazing contraptions. He didn't care for the yellow beasts in the land of the Orang Pendek that tore through the forest, but this contraption looked like fun. He spotted Pebble Nose sitting in one of the vessels and pointed her out to Songg. Then Songg gestured at Tick to follow him down the mountainside.

The yeti dropped on to all fours, using their knuckles for extra balance as they slipped through the forest – in and out of clusters of tree ferns. When the ground became steep, they tumbled down and shoulder-rolled, picking up speed along the forest floor, but leaving behind no sound greater than the whispering of the wind. They stopped on an overgrown outcrop that gave them a view of the human sett. Flittermouse swooped down and hung from a tree.

When the green contraption came to rest, Tick spotted

Pebble Nose getting out. Then, as she walked through the clusters of dwellings, Flittermouse followed, flying high above her head. The two yeti did their best to keep an eye on the tiny bat, tracking her from the hills above while staying in the shadows of the bush, hidden among the trees.

At last, Flittermouse returned to her friends, peeping and squeaking that she had indeed discovered the dwelling of Pebble Nose. The bat then led them along the hills to the outskirts of the human sett, and showed them the place.

Tick and Songg hid in the dense blades of flax and surveyed the dwelling at the base of the hill. It sat in a clearing hacked out of the bush, like a giant scab, a high barrier guarding its sides. The home had tall white walls and many openings covered with what looked like shining ice – a pool of water lay at the back.

Flittermouse chirped and shrilled.

"So the slabs are in the den that lies beneath the house – those openings there?" said Tick, pointing at the narrow slits at the side of the dwelling, just above the grass.

Flittermouse squeaked. She had already flown down for a closer look.

Songg let out a long sigh. "It's like a fortress. I fear we will never see those slabs again, Tick."

Tick shook his head. "I need to get them back, Songg,

even if it means breaking into that place."

"And what if the humans see you?" said Songg. "What if they manage to trap you – have you thought of that?" He gave a shudder.

"I know it's crazy, but I have to try." Tick turned to Flittermouse. "Did you see a doorway of any kind?"

Flittermouse said that she had – on the other side of the dwelling.

"Let's go back and join the others, tell them what we know, and see if we can come up with a plan," said Tick.

Songg snorted and headed back up the hill.

That evening, five yeti slipped through the trees under cover of darkness to return to the dwelling. Songg of the Makimaki and the four Mountain Yeti, with Flittermouse hovering close by.

Just think, all this could be over by morning, said the idea fly in Tick's ear.

The plan, as much as there was one, was to approach the human dwelling from the hills. Tick, Plumm and Dahl would slip inside, find the slabs in the den below ground and haul them away while Jiffi and Songg kept a lookout from the bush. Flittermouse would act as the advance party, flying ahead to make sure the way was clear.

The yeti waited and waited, Tick leaning into Jiffi's arms, and, when the moon had almost reached its highest point, the little lights around the dwelling went out until the place was in almost complete darkness.

"Let's go," commanded Dahl.

Jiffi reached for Tick's hand. "Good luck."

"Be safe," said Songg, unease in his eyes.

"Ready?" Tick asked Plumm.

The raiding party flowed through the bush with Dahl leading the way. He paused at the end of the treeline, before wading through the long grass that led to the high walls. The Guardian dropped down to his knees, his back to the wall. The others followed. They listened for a time, but there was only the sweet chirrup of crickets. Dahl motioned to the others and reached the top of the wall. He threw his Rumble Stick over first, then pulled himself to the top and rolled over to drop down on the other side. Tick and Plumm followed. Still nothing stirred in the dwelling.

The three yeti crept over the grass and sought shadows, Flittermouse flying ahead. Round the corner, they found stairs leading down to the doorway.

Here they paused, listening out for any signs of the humans, before padding down the stairs. Tick reached the doorway first. He took a deep breath. This was it. Just beyond this piece of wood lay the slabs. They would be in his hands very soon, and then everything would start to be right again.

Tick pushed against the wood. With a creak, the door swung open, revealing the darkened den – like a cave. As his eyes adjusted to the gloom, Tick made out what looked like some eating benches, and resting on them were the carvings. The slabs!

With quickening breath, Tick slipped into the den, fingers already reaching out, the others close behind.

A little red firefly winked at Tick from deep in the darkness – bright, like an ember. Then, all at once, a wailing, ear-splitting shriek screamed through the shadows. The din reached right into Tick's chest, rattling his heart. The young yeti dropped his staff and covered his ears. There was nothing else he could do. The raiding party stared at each other in sheer panic, and then they fled up the stairs and headed for the trees, Flittermouse flapping her wings as fast as she could.

The screeching of the alarm drove Ella from her bed. She scrambled free of the covers, heart pounding, and flicked on the light. As she opened the door, she saw Uncle Jack burst from his room in his pyjamas, a book in his hand.

"What's going on?" Ella cried.

Jack jabbed at the flashing alarm control panel on the wall of the hallway and then there was silence. "My studio!" he hissed, staring at the panel.

"The slabs!" gasped Ella. She was trembling. Had someone come to steal them? How would anyone even know they were here?

"Do we call the police?"

"I need to check the basement. Stay put."

Jack threw his book down on the table and rushed down the stairs two, at a time. Ella hesitated for a moment but then ran down after him.

Jack marched to the front door and slapped at a bank of switches, drenching the grounds around the house in light. He peered out into the gardens and grabbed an umbrella from the stand by the door.

"I don't see anyone," said Ella.

Jack frowned at her. "I thought I told you to stay put." He ran to the door that led down to the studio and opened it a crack. Then he shouted, "We're coming down and we're armed!"

There was no response, not a sound. Jack opened the door wide and crept down the stairs, Ella behind him. But the studio was deserted and everything appeared untouched. The slabs were exactly where Dr Milligan had left them. However, the outside door was wide open. Whatever had set off the alarm was long gone.

Jack shuffled over and locked the door. "Peeew. What is that smell?"

Ella sniffed. She felt the stench crawl up the back of her neck, making her hair stand on end. She recognized it instantly. From the mountains and from the hollow in the bush. It was a yeti smell. Yeti had been here!

"Possums?" she said quickly.

Jack sniffed the air. "A fairly pungent possum."

"Maybe Dr Milligan left the door open and a possum came in, looking for food. Lots of possums."

Jack didn't look convinced. "Could be, I suppose," he

said at last. "Nasty critters."

Then Ella saw a stick on the floor by Uncle Jack's feet – a straight tree branch – and rushed over to pick it up. She felt the smooth wood in her hands, brought it up to her nose and inhaled, quickly pulling back. It was a yeti staff, she was sure of it.

Just what was going on? The slabs had come all the way from the Himalayas. There was no way the yeti from the mountains could have come here, surely? But, if it wasn't them, then who? The yeti nearby? thought Ella. They could have done it. But how did they know the slabs were here?

She saw Uncle Jack staring at her. "The stick I picked up in the bush," Ella stammered. "I was wondering where I'd left it. The possums must have knocked it over."

"Don't go leaving your things lying all over the house, there's a good girl," said Jack. He double-checked he'd locked the door, tugging vigorously at the handle. Then he went from window to window, jerking at the latches. Satisfied at last, he gestured to Ella to go up the stairs.

On her way to her room, Ella spied Uncle Jack's book on the table. It was his yeti journal, the black notebook he'd checked all the time in the mountains. Ella picked it up. On the cover in neat writing was the name Ray Stevens. Ray Stevens – the explorer who took the yeti photo, the one who thought he saw yeti in the bushes nearby? Why did Uncle Jack have Stevens' journal?

Ella opened the book and began flipping through the pages. The journal was full of entries, maps, photographs and newspaper clippings. She read a few of the headlines:

YETI PHOTOGRAPH A HOAX!
YETI FINDINGS FAKED!
NZ EXPLORER A FRAUD!
EXPLORER'S SHAME...

The article about the hairy creature in Greyton was in there too. Then Ella came across the famous Stevens yeti photograph itself. It was grainy and the yeti was not much more than a haze – but the hairy back, the long arms... It was just like the yeti they'd seen in the mountains.

She turned to the last entry.

I just don't have the drive any more – I'm throwing in the towel. That's what the sceptics want. Their words still give me grief. But I know what I saw in the mountains and in the Greyton bush! I know the yeti are out there. They exist all over the world, I feel it in my heart.

I've spent a great deal of my life searching deep into the wilderness and, in the end, I am no closer to finding yeti than when I began. But perhaps that's just as well. What if I had discovered yeti? What then?

I just hope that, if someone finally unearths the truth, they treat the yeti with the dignity and care that they deserve, and not as animals in some circus.

I dreamed one day of contributing to science, but now I will leave all this behind and go back to the quiet life. To enjoying my home and the affection of my dear daughter Lucy, and little Deborah and Jack, my beloved grandchildren. As it should be.

Ray Stevens, 1971

A funny feeling came over Ella. She read the last line again. *Dear daughter Lucy, and little Deborah and Jack, my beloved grandchildren.*

Ella's grandmother Lucy had died before she was born.

Mum's name was Deborah. And Mum's older brother was Jack – Uncle Jack. Which would make Ray Stevens Ella's great-grandfather.

Can this night hold any more surprises? she thought.

★

The yeti strode through the forest, climbing uphill, seeking the deepest darkness where they could hide and keep a lookout. Songg slipped into a thick, low bush, the others behind him. Through the leaves, they could see the dwelling of the humans, now lit up as if it was in bright sun.

"Everyone OK?" asked Jiffi, panting. The others nodded.

"My ears are still ringing," said Tick.

"What on earth was that noise?" gasped Plumm.

"More human awfulness," Songg grunted. "Were you seen?"

Dahl shook his head. "I don't think so. The screaming began and we ran."

"I think it was an alarm," said Tick. "Like we blow in the sett to warn of danger. It came the moment I stepped inside the den. I saw a red firefly blink at me from the darkness – some sort of watch guard."

"The firefly must see if someone's coming and then start the noise," agreed Dahl.

Tick didn't think this was a good time to mention that he'd left his staff behind.

"What do we do now?" asked Plumm. "We can't get the slabs if that happens as soon as we set foot inside the place."

Dahl thought for a moment. "We'll stay close by tonight while we work out a new plan."

As soon as she woke up, Ella calculated the time difference in London – Mum and Dad's last stop – and called Mum. She didn't talk too long before she got to the point.

"It's been great spending time with Uncle Jack and getting to know him. It's made me think I should learn more about all my family – maybe make a family tree to share when I get back to school."

"That sounds like a great idea," said Mum.

"Thing is, I don't know much about the rest of them at all. Like, who was my great-grandfather?" asked Ella, holding her breath.

"OK," said Mum slowly. "You want to go that far back? My grandfather's name was Ray. Ray Stevens."

Ella gulped. "Not Stern?"

"No, my father's last name was Stern. Mum took his name when she married."

Ella clutched the phone. "What was your grandpa like?"

"I never really knew him that well, to be honest. I was a bit young. Grandpa Ray had been some kind of explorer back in the day, I think. But you should ask your Uncle Jack. He was the one who was close to him."

Ella's pulse quickened. "Uncle Jack, good idea."

"Listen, I've got to go, sweetie. We're on our way to a business dinner," said Mum. "But call me tomorrow, OK? We'll be back next week – can't wait to see you."

"Will do, Mum. Bye!"

Ella sat down on her bed with a thump. Ray Stevens, the discoverer of the yeti, was Mum and Uncle Jack's grandfather. So Jack must have learned all about yeti when he was growing up. And about how everyone labelled his grandfather a cheat.

So that's why he's so obsessed with finding the yeti, thought Ella. *He'll have a hit show as well, of course, but this isn't about wildlife or nature at all. Uncle Jack wants to clear Grandpa Ray's name.*

But Ella reckoned Grandpa Ray wouldn't have wanted his name cleared like this. He didn't want an animal circus – he'd said as much in his journal.

Ella needed to talk to Uncle Jack. She had to stop the yeti secrets from getting out.

"Ella!" Jack called from downstairs, startling her.

"Meeting in the studio now, please!"

She went down to the basement to find Dr Milligan, Ana and Walker already there. Jack was telling them about the alarm in the night.

"I'm not taking any chances. While your program works out the language of the slabs, I'm hiding them – putting them on lockdown," muttered Jack.

"Lockdown?" asked Ella.

"Yes, away from here, in the Rocky Hill Gun Tunnels."

"Those bunkers left over from World War Two? But they've been abandoned for years," said Ana. "Are they even still standing?"

"They were built to take a direct hit from a shell so I think they are. What's more, I managed to get the key."

"The conditions in there might damage the carvings," Dr Milligan grumbled.

"A concrete military bunker, empty and abandoned, just down the road and I have the key," said Jack. "Case closed. Now we shift them."

Ella watched as they trolleyed the carvings one by one up to Jack's gleaming SUV, with Dr Milligan fussing and tutting round them like a mother hen.

"Can we talk, Uncle Jack?" she asked.

Jack headed up the stairs. "Not now, Ella."

Outside, Ana and Walker rested the last of the slabs

in the back of the truck and Uncle Jack slammed the door.

"Take care, Mr Stern, take care!" moaned the doctor.

"Room for one more?" asked Ella.

"Sure," said Jack.

He drove them all out of town down a winding stretch of unsealed road. It didn't take long to find the bunkers, hulking and grey, perched on a hilltop facing the sea.

Jack swerved the car off the road and pulled to a stop on a square of gravel. They were outside a concrete block jutting out of the earth, sealed with a rusted iron door. He got out and strode up to the door, swinging the key on a piece of twine. Jack worked at the rusty padlock and the hinges wailed as he heaved the door open.

Just before they entered the tunnels, Ella bent down and grabbed some gravel, stuffing the stones into her pocket. They followed Jack into the dark, the torch beaming down the long shaft, the wheels of the trolley squeaking as Dr Milligan pushed. The gun tunnels were like a maze, Ella thought. Several times the group passed an intersection, where new tunnels branched left and right. Every few steps – and each time the path branched off – Ella reached into her pocket and dropped a pebble to the floor, marking a trail of their route.

They went on until Ella figured they must be deep in the heart of the hill. They passed open rooms, empty but for the bent remains of forgotten machinery.

At last, they reached a large room with AMMUNITION stencilled on the open door and Jack called them to a halt.

"This will do," he said. "Leave them in here."

26

The yeti lay low in the bush near the human dwelling, shaded by branches that spread over them like birds' wings. They had spent the night in the bush, taking turns to sleep and keep watch, but Tick felt his eyes had barely closed at all. When morning arrived, they kept their vigil, unsure what to do next. Tick gazed up at the treetops, watching a black bird with a tuft of white below its beak as it called sweetly across the forest.

There was a rustle in the bushes and Songg appeared with a handful of long, juicy worms. "Lunch!"

Jiffi scooped up a wriggling worm and popped it in her mouth. "Delicious."

The yeti ate silently, until there were no more left.

It was Plumm who spoke first. "Anyone have an idea how we're going to find the slabs now that they've moved them?"

Flittermouse chirruped.

"It's not your fault you couldn't fly as fast as the human contraption," said Tick. "I saw the way it sped down that road and got away. You tried your best."

"We need to be patient and keep our eyes on these humans. Something will come up," said Jiffi.

Tick sighed. "They must be so close to working out the secrets of the carvings by now."

★

Back in her room at Uncle Jack's, Ella lay on the bed and played with the phone in her hands, spinning it round and round. She just couldn't keep still.

Ana and the others had gone. Mum and Dad were wrapped up in their own world. Ella thought of messaging April about the yeti – but Jack had made them all promise not to tell anyone.

Ella dropped her phone on to the bedspread. She could smell the yeti staff from under the bed. She thought back to the night of the break-in. If the yeti had tried to raid the house, it meant they were desperate to get the slabs back. So just what was written on them? Ella decided to sneak down to the basement to take a look at Dr Milligan's translation program. Maybe there were some answers there. There hadn't been any further news since the skincare glitch.

Ella tiptoed downstairs and found the basement was deserted, no sign of Uncle Jack. She wiggled the mouse on Dr Milligan's computer and, when she saw the screen, she stopped cold.

And as the leaves and twigs and bark and branches and roots come together to make a tree, so it is with Earth. Everything united. And it is the solemn duty of every yeti to see that it remains so for ever more...

Ella read on, racing through the document, barely remembering to breathe.

Yeti were all over the world. They called themselves the Collective, all joined together by underground waterways. Ella kept scrolling. The writing talked about how yeti took care of pollination, fungus spreading, looking after animals and plants, fresh water, the ocean and so on and so on. There was barely a part of nature they didn't help. They were everywhere.

Ella remembered learning about how nature was like a delicate spider's web, everything connected. And how if you touched one thread you sent shudders through the whole thing. From what she was reading, yeti were the ones trying to keep the web intact!

Ella didn't dare think about what would happen if

humans found the yeti. It would ruin everything. There was more than these creatures at stake here and there was no more time to waste. She had to help them. But how?

The alarm had scared the yeti away but Ella doubted that they would just give up. The slabs meant too much to them. What would she do if she was in the same position?

"I'd hide close by and keep an eye on them," Ella said aloud.

The yeti might still be in the bush near the house! What if she took the bunker key and tried to make contact? If she turned up, carrying the staff, would they realize she meant no harm? Then she could guide the yeti to the Rocky Hill Gun Tunnels and lead them to the slabs, following her pebble trail. Ella smiled. That pebble trail was pretty clever.

But did she have the guts to do all that? Go behind Uncle Jack's back and ruin his lifelong dream? She fought the jumble in her head for a moment longer, then went back upstairs.

She found Uncle Jack in the living room, sipping coffee. She noticed the key to the tunnels sitting on the low table. "Uncle Jack, can we chat?"

Jack looked at his watch. "Not right this minute. I've got a conference call with the studio." He drained his coffee. "We'll talk later."

"But there's something I need to say."

"It'll have to wait, Ella. This is one of the biggest calls I've ever had to make – please understand. We're talking a potential three-series show here! We'll chat later, I promise," he said, disappearing into his office.

Ella sighed. "Well, at least I tried," she said to herself. She hesitated for a moment before grabbing the bunker key from the table where Jack had left it, and then went to get the staff from her room. Ella tiptoed past Uncle Jack's office and could hear he was already deep in conversation. She slipped out into the garden and up the slope towards the bush.

Once she reached a spot in full view of the hills, she laid the staff down on the grass. Then she took a few steps back and sat down. If they were here, they would come.

"You can't be serious," Songg hissed, his nostrils flaring. He glared at Pebble Nose sitting in the field below them. "To consort with a human? Do you know what the penalty is?"

"Banishment," said Tick and Jiffi together.

"Been there already," explained Jiffi.

"Me too," added Tick.

Dahl shifted in the undergrowth. "Look, I don't like

it any more than you, but we have to get the slabs back. What other choice do we have?"

"It's better for some of us to be discovered than for the location of every yeti sett on Earth to be revealed to the humans," said Tick. He gestured at Pebble Nose, who was still just sitting there. "Besides, Pebble Nose is different from the others. I think she means to help us."

"It could be a trick."

"It's a risk," acknowledged Tick.

Dahl handed Songg his Rumble Stick. "I want you to take this back to the sett. If anything should happen to us, see that it is returned to Greatrex."

"Back to the sett? But I'm coming with you," Songg replied.

Dahl shook his head. "This is a task for the Mountain Yeti. You need to keep the others on alert. If we should fail, you Makimaki may need to abandon sett. Agreed?"

"Agreed."

Tick pushed himself up to his feet. "I'll go down first and meet her. Stay hidden and wait for my signal."

"Be careful," said Plumm.

Tick pushed through the thicket, and stepped out into the open. Keeping his eyes on Pebble Nose, he strode down through the bush. When he reached the edge of the long grass, he crouched down. Tick stared the girl in the face, praying this wasn't a trap.

Ella got to her feet, her movements slow. She swallowed hard, her heart drumming in her chest. "Gentle, reclusive herbivore. Gentle, reclusive herbivore," she whispered to herself.

The yeti's head was large, like an orangutan. Dense brown fur covered his face, with a thick ridge running across the forehead. He had giant flared nostrils and dark, staring eyes. The eyes. Ella gulped. She had stared into them before. Up in the Himalayan forest. The yeti sitting in front of her right now was the same yeti she'd first seen! How had he got here? This was all too much.

Ella broke into a smile. The yeti tilted his head, then lifted his top lip to reveal a yellowing set of large teeth.

Please let that be a smile, thought Ella. Then she bent down to pick up the staff. "Stick... This is yours... Yours, stick," she managed to say, her voice quivering. As she was probably the first human to speak to a yeti, Ella wondered if she should have thought of something more impressive to say. She inched forward and held out the staff.

The yeti seemed to understand. He turned his head, looking towards the house, before getting up and reaching out for the stick. Ella shrank back. Now that he was standing close to her, she realized how huge the yeti was.

How strong the stink.

The yeti chortled something in a low voice.

"You're welcome," said Ella. She drew a square shape in the air, then turned to gesture over the hills in the distance. She mimicked carrying something heavy. She repeated the movements again.

The yeti nodded vigorously. With a thick finger, he pointed at his furry chest, and then at Ella.

Ella smiled back. "Yes," she said. "You need to come with me, and I'll take you to your slabs."

"Yerrsss."

The yeti scanned the field and the house again. When he seemed satisfied they were still alone, he turned and raised his staff high in the air.

Tick heard a rustle in the bushes behind him, then Dahl emerged, followed closely by the others. The yeti strode down to the field and joined Tick, squatting down in the coarse grass. Flittermouse flapped down and landed on Tick's shoulder.

"No sudden movements," said Tick. "It's got to be a little scary for her."

"She doesn't look scared," said Plumm, sniffing the air, trying to pick up the girl's scent. "They really don't smell of anything, do they?"

"Raise your lips and show her your teeth – smile the human way," said Tick.

"Now what?" said Plumm, her face fixed in a leer.

★

Now what? thought Ella. The pong that wafted towards her through the thick grass was enough to make her feel dizzy. There were four yeti crouched in the grass, and the first one had a bat on his shoulder. What Uncle Jack would do to be in her shoes! She wondered how long it would be before he discovered that both she and the key to the bunker were missing.

Ella saw that the yeti were all staring at her. She glanced at the dusty road. They would have to cross the hills and follow the road to the bunker from the bush, staying out of sight. The afternoon light was starting to fade – that would give them extra cover. Ella gestured to the yeti to follow her, before marching off across the field.

★

The yeti slunk through the grass, low to the ground, following Pebble Nose as she clambered over a low barrier towards the safety of the bush. Above their heads, Flittermouse squeaked.

"No sign of any humans up ahead," said Tick as the yeti

merged with the trees.

"I think this human means to stride the whole way," said Jiffi.

"At her pace? And have you ever heard anyone walk with so much noise?" Dahl gestured at Pebble Nose, who was scrambling over some fallen branches, twigs snapping and crunching.

"Humans," Plumm giggled.

"Then there's no choice," said Jiffi. "One of us will have to pick her up so we can stride properly."

"No fear," said Dahl.

"I'll do it," said Tick. "We're sort of friends after all."

"You won't even notice she's there. It'll be like carrying a sack of mulberries," laughed Plumm.

Tick called out to Pebble Nose. "Yerrsss!" The girl stopped, turned round and smiled.

"Ell-a," said Pebble Nose, pointing to herself. "Ell-a."

"Like the grunting of a yak," said Dahl.

"Ell-a," echoed Tick. He looked the girl over. She seemed so small and fragile. What if he dropped her? He'd just have to be careful. He pointed to the girl and to his shoulders. "Ell-a," he said again. "Yersss."

Ella remembered how Dad had carried her around on his shoulders all the time when she was little. It made sense, she supposed. She recalled just how fast this yeti was able to disappear into the distance up in the Himalayas.

The yeti handed his staff to one of the others. Then he scooped Ella up by her armpits as if she weighed nothing, lifted her high over his head and on to his furry shoulders. Ella tucked her calves under the yeti's arms for balance and gripped his fur – trying not to pull too hard. She decided it was probably best to avoid nostril-breathing for a while.

As soon as the yeti seemed satisfied that she was on securely, he began to run. Slowly at first but then gathering pace. Ella ducked down as they swept under branches. The yeti bounded through the bush, darting through the trees and gliding along the forest floor without once breaking his stride. The speed astounded Ella – it was like being on the back of a galloping horse. She laughed aloud.

They passed through a glade and Ella could see that they were straying from the road. She tapped the yeti on his arm and pointed.

"We need to go that way," she said.

The yeti nodded, and veered off in the right direction, the bat flapping above them. In the distance, Ella could see where the bush ended and the hills covered with boulders began. They'd be there in no time.

As the sun headed down towards the sea to the west, they reached the concrete bunker. At the edge of the treeline, the yeti paused. Ella couldn't see any sign of life near the front entrance. There were no cars parked there and no sound of anything coming down the road.

Ella pointed at the concrete box buried in the hill ahead. Her yeti friend nodded and set off at once, weaving through the boulders scattered over the hillside. At the iron gate, the yeti reached up and lifted Ella down.

Ella traced another square in the air with her fingers and pointed inside. Then she turned her attention to the padlock, working at it with the key. The lock resisted at first, but with a bit of wiggling it turned and Ella slid off the padlock, then pulled back the bolt. She grabbed the iron door in both hands and heaved it open. She held back for a moment, breathing in the musty tunnel air. Just a bit further, then the yeti would have their precious carvings back.

As the doorway groaned open, Tick peered into the long tunnel. He gave the sides of the passageway a poke with his finger. Hard as rock but with a surface that was smooth. It smelled dusty and lifeless. Nothing grew or lived down this tunnel. There was, however, the faintest of yeti odours coming from deep within. Tick's heart thumped – the slabs. Was this the moment when he got them back? Was a firefly light going to blink? Was there going to be the wail of an alarm horn?

Tick stepped inside the tunnel. Nothing happened. "Well, I guess this is it," he said.

"I worry this is all too convenient," said Dahl. "Once inside this cavern, we'll have no way of escape. *A ripe fruit is often full of worms.*"

"The whole time on the stride over here, she's been at our mercy. She's taken as much of a risk as us. We can trust her," Tick pointed out.

"Jiffi, can you hide near this entrance and keep a lookout?" asked Dahl.

"Of course."

Dahl continued. "Flittermouse, you travel further up the human road and watch for their contraptions. Warn Jiffi at the first sight of anything. Tick, Plumm and I will go in and rescue the slabs."

Flittermouse shrilled a quick goodbye and flapped away.

Tick took another deep sniff. "But how will we see in there?"

From Ella's hand came a sudden burst of light. The yeti took a step back. It was almost if she'd understood what they were saying, but then Tick knew that wasn't likely.

"Wow, this human girl is amazing," said Plumm, gazing in wonder at the beam of light that shot out down the tunnel. "How does she even do that?"

"Brighter than any firefly lamp," admitted Dahl.

The yeti watched as Ella crept into the tunnel, following the beam.

"See you soon, Mum," said Tick, handing Jiffi his staff. "We'll have the slabs before you know it."

★

Ella pointed the torch on her phone down the shaft. When she came up to the first pebble she'd thrown earlier that day, she grinned. It was a small thing to be so pleased about, but that pebble was ridiculously comforting. When she passed another little stone, Ella began to walk faster, confident now she knew what she was doing. As she and the yeti walked, the only sound coming down the tunnel was her own footsteps. The pebble trail turned to the right, then carried on past some empty rooms.

At last, they reached the room where the slabs were stored. Ella pushed open the door and stood back. The yeti filed in without waiting. At the sight of the carvings resting on the floor of the room in a tidy pile, they began to gurgle to each other, running their fingers over the surfaces.

"Yersss, Ell-a," said the yeti who'd carried her.

★

"Let's go," said Dahl, wasting no time. "Tick, you and Plumm grab one side of the slabs. I'll take the other."

Tick, Plumm and Dahl bent down at the knees and took up the slabs. With a slight groan, they lifted them off the ground. The weight of them didn't enter Tick's mind. All he could think was that the slabs were finally back in his hands. That, after all they'd been through, the sett and the Collective could go back to normal.

Then two things happened: first, the light in Ell-a's

hand dimmed and went out, followed by Jiffi's worried voice barrelling down the maze of tunnels. "Humans! Humaaaaans!"

"On our way!" Dahl bellowed down the shaft. "Quick, quick! As fast as you can!"

"But I can't see a thing!" said Plumm.

Tick felt Ell-a take hold of his fur, and he started stumbling backwards, his hands gripping the carvings tightly. "Ell-a will guide us."

Ella didn't need to know any yeti to understand the alarm in the lookout's voice. Someone was coming – and she had a pretty good idea just who that someone was. What a time for the phone battery to die. It was so dark inside the tunnel that she couldn't even tell if her eyes were open or not. The tunnels seemed to close in around her and, for the first time that day, Ella was terrified.

With one hand on the fur of her yeti friend behind her, she felt the wall of the corridor with the other, dragging her shoe along the tunnel floor to feel for the pebbles. At the first intersection, she gave the yeti a shove that said 'stop' and felt her way round the corner until she discovered another pebble. Then she hurried back to grab hold of him again.

At last, it seemed as if the gloom started to lighten.

The tunnel entrance. Ella thought she could see a hulking shape blocking the way, but it was hard to tell against the evening sky.

★

"Hurry, for fungi's sake – they're here, they're here!" Jiffi shouted.

"How far?" Tick yelled back.

A sound of crunching stones, the growl of a human contraption and a flash of bright light – like a beacon of fire – gave him the answer. The humans had arrived.

"Come on!" yelled Dahl.

★

Ella stumbled from the tunnel first, glad to be out of the concrete tomb. She shielded her eyes from the glare of headlights. She could make out the shape of her uncle, with Ana and Walker beside him. Was Uncle Jack holding a rifle?

"Yeti!" cried Jack. "Good grief! Ella, what the heck is going on? Stay where you are!"

"I don't believe it! Yeti!" Walker gasped, his camera blinking. "Rolling!"

"Everyone keep calm!" said Ana.

"Come away, Ella," Jack barked. "You'll be safe with us."

"They're not dangerous. They just want what belongs to

them," Ella pleaded.

"You're not thinking straight. Come over here," said Jack.

"No," said Ella. She felt her eyes fill with tears.

★

"Come on, we can still do this – we just need to get away from the light," Tick whispered. "When I say, we start running up the hill."

"No, nobody move," growled Dahl. "He's holding a thunderclap! He had one up in the mountain. I've heard it roar."

★

"That one is growling – he's growling!" Jack gulped and raised his rifle. "Move aside!"

Ana turned on Jack. "Put that gun down, Jack! Someone's going to get hurt."

Jack swung his rifle from one yeti to another. "Ella, get out of the way! Look at the size of them!"

"But Unc—" cried Ella as Ana made a lunge for the rifle.

★

The thunderclap sounded. Dahl let out a roar and dropped the slabs.

Tick watched as the humans wrestled each other, fighting over the thunderclap. "Go! To the trees!" he shouted as they reached down and lifted the slabs back up. Tick lurched up the hill, dragging Plumm and Dahl with him, all of them wheezing under the weight of the carvings.

"I'm wounded," Dahl gasped.

Jiffi ran to his side, and lifted the carvings. "I've got them – take the staff and go!" she cried.

Dahl pushed on into the darkness, stumbling towards the hillside, using Tick's staff as a crutch, dragging his leg behind.

"Did the thunderclap get you?" gasped Tick as they stumbled up the hill.

"No, the carvings fell on my foot."

Tick heard Flittermouse hovering in front of him. "This way!" Tick called out.

"I think they're chasing us again!" Plumm cried. "We can't outrun them."

"Oh yes we can," said Tick.

"Too heavy – we must leave the slabs," said Jiffi.

"No!" Dahl snapped. "We cannot let the humans get them again. There's too much at stake."

"There's no other way," Jiffi puffed.

All of a sudden, the idea fly buzzed to life in Tick's head. *Yes there is!*

"Put the slabs down, all of you. I'll make sure the humans don't get them," Tick ordered.

Plumm and Jiffi stared at Tick – but there was something in his voice that made them listen. Quickly, they laid the slabs on the ground.

"Mum, you help Dahl back to the sett," said Tick. "Flittermouse, you go with them. Plumm, you stay with me."

Trust me, said the idea fly.

"The humans will not get these slabs," Tick repeated.

"I hope you know what you're doing," Dahl said, then he and Jiffi struggled on, Flittermouse hovering above them.

Now pick up one of those boulders, said the fly.

Tick grabbed a rock and lifted it above his head. He took a long, deep breath. What he was about to do was unspeakable. They had travelled so far and gone through so much to get the slabs back. He was looking at a fate worse than banishment, if there was such a thing. Tick brought the boulder down with a crack!

Rock met stone with a crunch, sending rock splinters flying into the bush.

"Tick!" Plumm gasped. "What are you doing?"

"Making sure the humans don't get them." Tick picked the boulder back up and brought it crashing down.

Plumm hesitated, but then she reached for her own

stone and joined in – the two yeti rained down blow after blow, pulverizing the slabs. There would be no deciphering them now. Then they dropped their rocks and moved fast, striding for the trees.

★

Ella scrambled up the hillside, chasing after Uncle Jack as he ran after the yeti, the rifle still in his hands.

"You're not getting away!" yelled Jack into the gloom at the fleeing yeti. He raised the rifle to his shoulder.

"No!" Ella shouted.

"Go away, Ella!"

"Grandpa Ray wouldn't want this!"

At the sound of Ray's name, Jack paused.

"Grandpa Ray would tell you to stop," said Ella.

Slowly, Uncle Jack lowered the rifle. He turned to face Ella. "What do you know about Grandpa Ray?" he muttered.

"I read his journal. I found it in your house." Ella swallowed, trying to catch her breath. "Grandpa Ray wanted the yeti to be treated with care – it was the last thing he wrote. He was interested in the yeti species, not a yeti circus. He would never have used a gun!"

"But Ella—"

"You wanted to clear his name by finding proof but you've lost sight of what matters. Nature, wildlife, the way you used to care for animals. Showing the yeti to the world will just ruin everything, even if it does make you a massive hit show."

Ana caught up to them on the hillside, Walker puffing and panting behind her.

"The yeti?" asked Ana, peering into the dark.

Jack stood silent for a moment, panting. "Gone," he said at last, his voice just a whisper.

Ana saw the pile of crushed gravel. "They've smashed up their carvings too!"

"Well, it doesn't matter. We've got proof that yeti exist right here." Walker held up his camera. "Everything OK, Jack?"

Jack slung the rifle over his shoulder. "Everything's just fine. Come on. Let's go home."

28

Later that night, once they'd reached the sett with news of their daring raid, the yeti celebrated. The Makimaki cooks prepared a vast feast, boiled in the scalding blast of a steam vent: centipedes and wild rice, rabbit-dropping dumplings with nuts, mussels and roots. The meeting hall echoed with laughter and good cheer. Then, when the last of the food disappeared, the light of flickering lanterns dropped down low, and the steady twang of instruments began.

The Makimaki pushed back the eating benches and danced, the music growing fast and frantic. Plumm grabbed Tick by the hands, and pulled him from the crowd, and, before he could say no, he was twirling and stomping with the rest of them.

"Enough, enough," laughed Tick when he could dance no more. He let go of Plumm's hands.

"Spoilsport," teased Plumm, sticking out her tongue.

They wandered over to where Jiffi and Dahl were talking with Songg.

"You did so well on our mission," said Jiffi, ruffling her son's hair. "You set out to get the slabs from the humans and you did just that. I couldn't be prouder."

"All my life I have protected the slabs, upheld what's written," Dahl grumbled. "After all we've been through to get them back, and you and Plumm go and smash them to pieces."

"I'm sorry, Dahl, but I could see no other way."

Dahl chortled. "I'm just teasing. You did well for a pair of younglings."

"Wow! I wasn't expecting you to say that."

"This journey, the trials we have faced, the yeti we have met…" Dahl took Jiffi's hand, "…your mum's story. There's great wisdom in the slabs, and much to value – that is certain. But I'm starting to believe that our paths through life should live and breathe, rather than stay set in ancient stone. There's a scent of change in the air. Perhaps you've done us all a favour, Tick."

"Not bad for an exile," said Jiffi.

The Makimaki musicians started a new tune, setting off on a wild rhythm. "How about a dance?" Jiffi prodded Dahl in the arm.

"I would if it wasn't for this bad leg," said Dahl.

"Clumsy oaf," said Jiffi.

"Come on," laughed Plumm, grabbing Songg's arm.

Tick watched the others dance for a bit and then drifted from the cavern. While the party was going on, there was something he still had to do. "Come on, Flittermouse," Tick said to the little bat clinging to his fur. "We have an errand to run."

Tick followed the tunnel uphill and out into the cave which opened up on to the bush. He paused for a moment, sniffing the air for intruders, then listened for the heavy footfall of the humans. There was nothing but crickets and the haunting cry of a lonely owl. Flittermouse stretched her wings and flew off into the darkness.

Tick followed his bat friend through the trees as she headed down the hillside towards the human dwelling of the slab stealers. Once it was in sight, Tick sat in the bushes for a time, checking the land outside to see that there were no humans about – no little red glows of the screaming alarm, no nasty surprises. Apart from the light coming from the bottom of the dwelling, the place looked deserted.

Tick crept up to the entrance and there he laid down his staff. Then he turned and ran for the safety of the bush, Flittermouse soaring above.

★

The film crew and Ella gathered in the studio, which somehow seemed forlorn without the slabs.

"Now perhaps you'd better tell us everything you know," said Jack.

Ella sighed. She was glad to get it out in the open – it had been hard sneaking around and keeping secrets all this time. Ella told the others how she worked out that the slab map showed where yeti could be found all over the world, including New Zealand – she told them about the newspaper article she dug up about Ray Stevens that led her to think about searching the bush nearby. She explained about her train trips, and the rock stack, and the smell. Ella described finding the yeti staff on the night of the break-in, proving that they'd been there. She explained how she'd realized just how intelligent the yeti really were.

"Investigated like a true field naturalist," said Ana.

Ella blushed.

"So Grandpa Ray was right about them being in these hills. Everyone thought he was nuts." Jack sighed. "I believed in him, though."

"Well, I guessed the yeti would come looking again – they had to – so this afternoon I took the staff and I went out to find them," said Ella.

Walker whistled. "It was a big gamble – you had no idea what you could have been up against."

"Ana said they were most probably gentle creatures,

and I trust her," said Ella. "There's more. I brought you down to the studio to look at this, before Dr Milligan comes back and gets a chance to see it." Ella tapped the keyboard, bringing the screen to life. "His program finally translated the yeti's language. I saw it this afternoon."

She read out aloud. "*In the beginning came Earth Mother, the first of the striders, the first of our kind. Earth Mother told her children to stride over mountain and ocean, and where they journeyed so they dwelled. And so the Collective began...*"

The others read on, shaking their heads in disbelief.

"They do all these amazing things, all over the planet," said Ella.

Walker whistled. "Imagine the online storm this would make. It would break the internet."

"And what would happen to the yeti after that?" asked Ella. "No more yeti, no more yeti help."

Jack hung his head, and at last he let out a long sigh. "I guess I've been blinkered this whole time."

"You're not the only one," said Ana. She gave Ella an apologetic smile.

"I was only thinking of my huge discovery. I was so close too," said Jack.

"Closer than anyone ever got – that's something," said Ella.

"True."

"So what now?" asked Ana.

"Let the yeti get back to what they were doing before any of this started," said Jack.

Ella's face broke into a wide grin.

"But first there are some yeti tracks to cover up, starting with this." Jack opened Walker's camera and took out the memory card. He held it in his fingers and let out a long breath, before throwing it on the floor and crushing it with his shoe. Walker winced.

Ella leaned over and made several clicks with the mouse. "Now there's no camera footage, no carvings and no file."

"I think the yeti will just have to be our little secret," said Jack.

Walker smiled. "What yeti?"

"Well, that's that," said Ana. "I'd better let Dr Milligan know the slabs were vandalized in the night and coincidentally a virus has wiped all his work – that'll take some telling."

"I'll phone the studio tomorrow," said Jack, turning to go back upstairs. "With zero to show for all these expeditions, they'll pull the plug, no question. My yeti obsession was hanging by a thread anyway. On the upside, I've got a feeling we could all be back for another series of *Stern Stuff* soon enough," Jack said to Ana and Walker. "Did you know it's had over four million views?"

The Mountain Yeti and the Makimaki faced each other on the bank of the underground stream. It was time to say goodbye.

Flittermouse was to return to her kin with the Mande Barung and pass on the message: the slabs were no longer in human hands. All was well. Keep safe.

Tick tickled the tiny bat under her chin for the last time. "I don't do long goodbyes," he stammered, his voice breaking. "Thanks for everything, dear friend. *May the wind be always at your back.*"

Flittermouse nuzzled into Tick's fur and trilled.

"Yes, I'm sure our paths will cross again too," said Tick.

Flittermouse unfurled her wings, flew down the tunnel towards the cave entrance and was gone.

"It's not just Flittermouse that has many moons' travel ahead of her," said Dahl.

The yeti all raised their arms, touching their chests and then their heads in silent salute.

"*One shall not reach the top of a mountain by sitting on the bottom*," intoned Dahl, bowing.

"There is part of us that shall always be Makimaki," said Jiffi.

The four yeti clambered into the canoe. "Perhaps we shall return to visit one moon," Dahl grunted as he untied the rope, and pushed off from the bank.

"Or perhaps we'll come to your place," said Dunkk.

"Till then." Dahl called to Jiffi sitting at the front. "Ready, navigator?"

"Stick to the right, and then it's the second tunnel on the left," Jiffi called.

"No problem," said Tick.

Jiffi dipped her paddle into the water, setting the stroke, the others following. The boat floated away into the dark, the soft sound of a Makimaki farewell song pushing them on…

★

The great fungusatory was full of commotion and bustle. On the cave floor, teams of yeti worked the fungus fields – spades and rakes in hand, planting new spores, gathering those that were grown, spreading compost. Water carriers passed the waterwheel in procession, picking up full buckets. Basket after basket of fungus was lifted up to the ceiling on ropes, ready to be scattered on the wind.

Tick looked round the farm. He couldn't believe he'd missed it so much. To be near a larder full of pine-needle cake and slug jam. To hear bark paper pages rustling in the library, and the flonking pit echoing to the sound of chanting and cheers as sopping dwiles found their mark. After all they'd done to protect the slabs, the elders had ruled that Tick and his mum were no longer exiles. He'd gone back to being *(he with no time to waste)* and Jiffi was once again *(she always in a hurry)*. Dahl had made sure of that. Everything was as it should be.

After last horn, Tick left the fungusatory and padded back along the tunnels to his den. He pushed the moss curtain aside to find his new denmate hanging a daisy chain around her neck. At the sight of her son, Jiffi smiled – a big human smile with plenty of teeth.

"They look nice," said Tick, pointing to her flowers. He looked round his den. It felt so much better now Mum was back. The carpet of lichen seemed softer beneath his feet and there was a warmth to the place that hadn't been present before. There wasn't a gnawing, nagging sense of misgiving hanging in the air. For the first time, this funny little den felt like home. Mum was back, Tick realized with a grin. She truly was.

★

At the Sasquatch sett, Inke led the volunteers in their daily training. Half a dozen yeti struggled their way up vines, hand over hand, their big feet pushing, their hairy legs swaying.

"Incoming!" yelled Grubb as a bat swooped down. Inke held his arm out for the bat to latch on to. The fruit bat squeaked its news.

"The secret of the slabs safe ... maintain vigilance ... invitation ... Collective gathering ... location to be confirmed..." said Grubb.

Spratt slid down the vine. "Good news, sir?"

"Very good news," said Inke. "Make ready the craft. Have Ranke gather supplies. Prepare to move out at short notice!"

★

Sipp, leader of the Almas, was feeding a herd of argali sheep, their horns large and curved, when the messenger arrived.

"Planke, Aspp, Gagg!" she called out after hearing everything the bat had to say. "Our friend brings news. All is safe. The Collective meets again."

"Tremendous!" said Planke.

"We'll need a big boat," added Aspp, eyeing the sheep.

Crisp bobbed in the ocean, a sack of coral spore at his side. Shrubb trod water close by.

"You about done?" asked Shrubb.

"Last of them now, sis," said Crisp, releasing another handful of the tiny red dots.

Shrubb began swimming back to the beach with steady strokes. A tiger shark slunk out of the shadows and glided towards her hairy legs. Shrubb thumped it on the nose. "Silly fish," she chuckled.

As the Yowie climbed out on to the sand, their fur sodden and dripping, a bat flew above their heads three times, before latching on to a nearby branch.

"Another bat friend!" said Crisp. The Yowie listened to the messenger's squeaks.

"Wow, the Collective is getting back together. We'd better go and tell the others," Shrubb whistled. "Do you think we'll get to go?"

"It's probably just elders."

"Probably," said Crisp.

★

"A Collective gathering, well, that is good news," said Shipshape of the Greybeards. "We ought to offer to host it. I'll send word."

"A fine idea," agreed Rainstorm. "It's been a long time since we all met. Not in my lifetime anyway."

"Just goes to show that some good can come out of a crisis," said Shipshape. "You know what they say: *when the going gets hairy, the hairy get going.*"

★

"So what was your trip like?" said April. "I loved all those photos you shared with me." There were still a few minutes before first bell and excited first-day chatter filled the hallway.

"It was awesome. I went right up into the Himalayan mountains with the film crew."

"Wow. I wish I had a famous uncle like you."

Ella smiled. "Yeah, Uncle Jack's OK."

"So are you going to be on TV?"

"The programme never got made in the end. There were a few problems."

"That's a shame," said April.

"Real shame," agreed Ella. "But Uncle Jack's already doing another season of *Stern Stuff*, though."

"Love that show," said April.

The bell clanged, and hundreds of blue uniforms began filing their way into the classrooms.

"Goodbye, holiday," said Ella with a sigh.

She and April made their way into English class and

found two desks at the back. Written on the whiteboard was:

Write two paragraphs about an interesting thing you did or saw over the summer.

"Great, two paragraphs about my game console," said April. "What about you, Miss I-went-to-the-Himalayas?"

Ella pictured the campsite by the river, the trek through the forest. She remembered the yeti – the wonderful, magical yeti – the slabs, the chase at the gun tunnels. She'd helped save the yeti – she'd always have that. And there was the wooden staff, worn smooth by the hands of her friend, resting in her closet.

"Yak," said Ella. "I'm going to write about yak."

EPILOGUE

Tick and Plumm waved goodbye to the sentry yeti guarding the north entrance, and squeezed through the gap between the boulder and the side of the mountain.

"Make sure you're back by sunset," said one.

"Nice job you did with that whole rescue thing," said the other.

"Thanks," said Tick.

The two yeti took deep breaths of the fresh mountain air. There was the strong scent of pine from the forest, with a touch of sap.

"Come on," said Plumm, striding down the hillside. "These bags need filling."

Tick caught up with her and the two of them flowed through the shadows. Nosh wanted lots of wild thyme and rosemary, which grew in bunches in the rocky soil at the base of the mountain. The yeti took the trail to the herb garden, following their noses.

"I'm surprised they trust me out here at all, after what happened last time," said Tick, taking a break from picking herbs to turn his face to the sun. "Mind you, I'm completely over my human thing."

"What about Ell-a?" teased Plumm.

Tick gave her a shove. "But you know what she did help to prove? People aren't all bad. Mum was right all along."

"Have you noticed how Dahl is more relaxed since we came back?"

Tick chewed on a twig of rosemary. "Not just Dahl but Greatrex too. Itch told me he even overheard them talking about getting some new slabs for the sett carved the other moon. Greatrex said it might be time for changes."

"Changes?"

"Yeah, a look at rewriting some of the rules. Dahl has been whispering in his ear. He reckons we could learn things from some of the other setts too. Greatrex has requested a Collective gathering. Word's already gone out."

"Gathering? Where?"

"I think it's at the sett of the Greybeards. A long way off in the lands to the north. Itch told me."

"New rules? Not sure Nagg will like that," murmured Plumm, tying up her sack. She prodded Tick in the arm. "You finished gathering or what?"

The two yeti climbed back up the mountainside, stopping to eat a pine cone or two along the way. As they reached the top of the mountain, something fluttering in the trees caught Tick's eye. It was a piece of paper impaled on one of the branches. It looked like human paper, blown there on the wind.

Go and get it, said the idea fly. *You never know what it might be.*

Tick laid down his new staff. "Just a second." He took hold of the tree trunk and pulled himself up, and then went hand over hand along the branch, the wood straining under his weight, until his fingers grasped the shred of paper. With a tug, it came loose and Tick dropped to the ground.

"What is it?" asked Plumm.

Tick couldn't read what it said, so he folded the paper. He would show it to Greatrex. "Let's go," he said. "Nosh will be wondering about her herbs."

When asked, as I frequently am, why I should concern myself so deeply with the conservation of animal life, I reply that I have been very lucky and that throughout my life the world has given me the most enormous pleasure. But the world is as delicate and as complicated as a spider's web. If you touch one thread, you send shudders running through all the other threads. We are not just touching the web, we are tearing great holes in it.

Gerald Durrell, 1925–1995

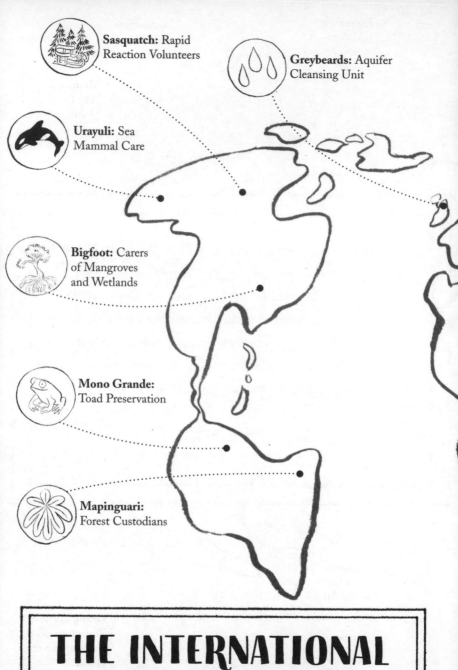

Sasquatch: Rapid Reaction Volunteers

Greybeards: Aquifer Cleansing Unit

Urayuli: Sea Mammal Care

Bigfoot: Carers of Mangroves and Wetlands

Mono Grande: Toad Preservation

Mapinguari: Forest Custodians

THE INTERNATIONAL YETI COLLECTIVE

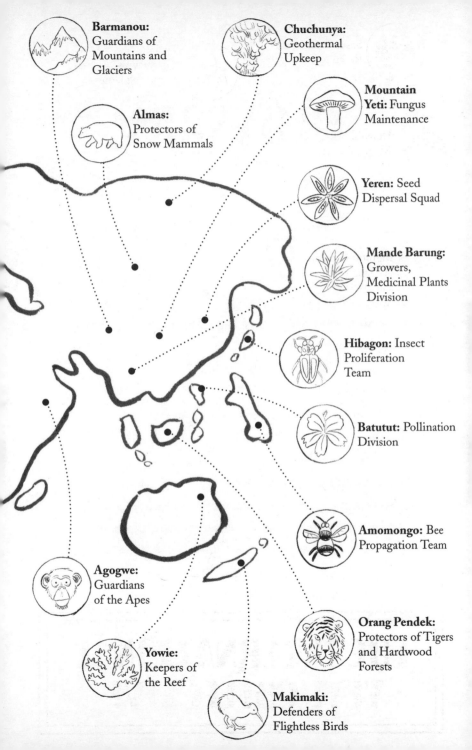

Barmanou: Guardians of Mountains and Glaciers

Chuchunya: Geothermal Upkeep

Almas: Protectors of Snow Mammals

Mountain Yeti: Fungus Maintenance

Yeren: Seed Dispersal Squad

Mande Barung: Growers, Medicinal Plants Division

Hibagon: Insect Proliferation Team

Batutut: Pollination Division

Amomongo: Bee Propagation Team

Agogwe: Guardians of the Apes

Orang Pendek: Protectors of Tigers and Hardwood Forests

Yowie: Keepers of the Reef

Makimaki: Defenders of Flightless Birds

GLOSSARY

Banishment: being sent to live far away from the sett
Cocoon: a human tent
Council of Elders: the ruling body of the sett; the cabinet
Denmate: roommate
Earth Mother: in yeti mythology, the first of the yeti
Firebird: helicopter
Fledgling: infant or toddler
Flonking: a game where the opponents aim to splat each other with a sopping rag. Practised in some places by humans too
Fungusatory: the fungus farm
Guardian: protector of the sett
Leaf Yeti: the giver of names in the yeti naming ceremony. Not dissimilar to the Burryman, an ancient human tradition

Rumble Stick: the staff and symbol of the Guardian

Scatterer Yeti: the yeti who spread the fungus over the forest

Sett: the yeti home and community

Silverback: the leader of the sett

Staunch Veil: the secret Mountain Yeti stronghold, used in times of crisis

The Collective: the group of nineteen yeti setts around the world

The slabs: the precious laws, legends and history of the yeti

Thunderclap: rifle, gun

Tree-striding: running through the forest, silent and unseen, leaving no trace behind

Youngling: child

ACKNOWLEDGEMENTS

I finished my first draft of *The International Yeti Collective* back in 2014 (has it really been that long?) and have watched it grow and develop over the years into the book now resting in your hands. This would not have happened without the support and involvement of the following people:

Rachel Boden, who warmly accepted the yeti into the Stripes family; Ella Whiddett, Sophie Bransby and Leilah Skelton at Stripes; my copy editor, Jane Tait; Barbara Else at the TFS literary agency; Roz Hopkins and Natalie Winter at Captain Honey; my father David for reading draft after draft, and for always being willing to lend me his insight; my trusted critics: my children Mia and Miles, and my wife Jenny (who have probably heard enough about yeti to last a lifetime) and cousin Joe for his encouragement, and for helping me imagine how the yeti might look.

I would also like to thank the Driving Creek Railway for all the inspiring train rides through the bush over the years, and countries all around the world for their yeti folklore as well as some wonderful proverbs, sayings and wisdom.

I am especially thrilled to share these pages with the talented Katy Riddell and see her warm and thoughtful pen-and-ink drawings bring the yeti to life.

And last but certainly not least, I owe an enormous debt to Ruth Bennett, my editor, whose intuition, advice and unwavering belief have been instrumental in shaping this book and driving it forward. Thank you.

– Paul Mason

ABOUT THE AUTHOR

Inspired by his own family and by his time as a primary
school teacher, Paul Mason likes to write stories that get
young readers turning pages. His published work crosses
a range of genres, and includes *The Twins, the Ghost
and the Castle* and the *Skate Monkey* series. He lives
on an island in Aotearoa New Zealand, and can be
found with a little book and a fountain pen in
his hands, catching ideas before they disappear.

ABOUT THE ILLUSTRATOR

Katy Riddell grew up in Brighton and was obsessed
with drawing from a young age, thanks to growing up
in a house of artists, including award-winning illustrator
Chris Riddell. Since graduating with a BA Hons in
Illustration and Animation from Manchester Metropolitan
University, Katy has worked on a variety of commissions
including *Pongwiffy* by Kaye Umansky and
Midnight Feasting by A.F. Harrold.

More adventures of
THE INTERNATIONAL
YETI COLLECTIVE...

COMING SOON!